Pr...

UNIVERSE

'Sibéal Pounder's books are the most fought over in our house. They've brought so much joy and laughter, and *Neon's Secret UNIverse* is no exception. Fun, funny, magical and fizzing with imagination, my children and I have been pinching it off each other since it landed!'
Sophie Anderson, author of
The House with Chicken Legs

'I adored not-at-all normal Neon and her madcap adventure'
Joanna Nadin, author of
The Worst Class in the World series

'*Neon's Secret UNIverse* is exactly what the world needs right now: a glorious, galloping, life-affirming stampede of pure multicoloured joy. I want to go on holiday inside Sibéal Pounder's head'
Chris Smith, author of
Kid Normal, The Great Dream Robbery and
Frankie Best Hates Quests

'Bright, bubbly and never knowingly normal, *Neon's Secret UNIverse* is a whirlwind of witty, wonderful adventure!'
Mo O'Hara, author of
My Big Fat Zombie Goldfish and *Agent Moose*

Books by Sibéal Pounder

Neon's Secret UNIverse
Neon and the Unicorn Hunters

Tinsel: The Girls Who Invented Christmas

Bad Mermaids
Bad Mermaids: On the Rocks
Bad Mermaids: On Thin Ice
Bad Mermaids Meet the Sushi Sisters
Bad Mermaids Meet the Witches (for World Book Day)

Witch Wars
Witch Switch
Witch Watch
Witch Glitch
Witch Snitch
Witch Tricks

Beyond Platform 13 (with Eva Ibbotson)

SIBÉAL POUNDER

Illustrated by Sarah Warburton

BLOOMSBURY
CHILDREN'S BOOKS
LONDON OXFORD NEW YORK NEW DELHI SYDNEY

BLOOMSBURY CHILDREN'S BOOKS
Bloomsbury Publishing Plc
50 Bedford Square, London WC1B 3DP, UK
29 Earlsfort Terrace, Dublin 2, Ireland

BLOOMSBURY, BLOOMSBURY CHILDREN'S BOOKS
and the Diana logo are trademarks of Bloomsbury Publishing Plc

First published in Great Britain in 2023 by Bloomsbury Publishing Plc

A catalogue record for this book is available from the British Library

ISBN: PB: 978-1-4088-9416-3; eBook: 978-1-4088-9415-6; ePDF: 978-1-5266-6182-1

2 4 6 8 10 9 7 5 3 1

Typeset by RefineCatch Limited, Bungay, Suffolk
Printed and bound in Great Britain by CPI Group (UK) Ltd, Croydon CR0 4YY

To find out more about our authors and books visit www.bloomsbury.com
and sign up for our newsletters

For Jim
– S.P.

For Fiona, Denise and Debbie (the Witches), who
help me with the crazier stuff in life!
– S.W.

UHs Stands for UNICORN HUNTERS!

My name is Priscilla Knackerman and I just want to say: I am a Unicorn Hunter! That's right, I'm an UH. Pronounced like you would say 'uuuh?'

The UHs are as old as ... really old stuff! And we know the truth about unicorns. They are NOT horses with horns, that's just something they made up to distract us. The truth is, unicorns are the most powerful beings on the planet – more powerful than witches or mermaids or elves, and they look just like you and me! You'd never spot one unless you knew what to look for: a stripe of colourful hair at the back of their head. They live in a secret world known as the UNIverse. It's impossible to get there unless you find a portal opener. Rumour has it the last surviving portal opener is hidden

1

right here in Brunty. And I'm going to find it! It's what I was born to do – find a portal to the UNIverse, jump in and DESTROY THE UNICORNS!

Now, I'd better go because tomorrow is an exciting day. We're going to go digging for the portal opener, plus we have new neighbours moving in. My mum said the girl is my age! She's called Neon Gallup. I bet we become BEST FRIENDS.

One Week Later

1

Priscilla Knows

December 1996, two months since Priscilla Knackerman discovered Neon has the portal opener and saw her jumping into the UNIverse.

Neon Gallup dragged an old, battered green lipstick across her bedroom wall and watched as the mark she'd made fizzed and crackled and began to rip open.

This was Neon's big secret. She had found the lipstick when she moved into her new house, hidden in a secret compartment in the window sill. It had been covered in goo and turned out not to be just any old lipstick – it was a lipstick that opened a portal to the UNIverse! The secret world where *real* unicorns live.

Neon took a step back as a tidal wave of glitter burst

from the portal and shot across the floor. Beyond the rip she could see the colourful world of the UNIverse glittering in sunlight.

No one knew she had a secret life, in a secret world. No one knew she had become a UNICORN! She touched the stripe of green in the back of her hair.

No one knew her secret!

OR DID THEY?

Though Neon didn't know it, two months earlier her new neighbour Priscilla Knackerman had walked into Neon's room at the exact moment she was jumping through the portal to the UNIverse! Priscilla had SCREAMED, and Neon would've screamed too had she seen her, because not long ago Neon had discovered Priscilla is a UNICORN HUNTER! The scariest creatures on the planet, if you're a unicorn. But Neon didn't see Priscilla that day and Priscilla didn't run and tell anyone Neon's secret – or at least not yet anyway. She didn't inform the UHs that she knew where the portal opener was. She didn't mention that Neon was a unicorn. She didn't do anything. For some strange reason, Priscilla didn't tell *anyone* …

Neon clambered through the portal and landed with a thud in the capital city of Lumino, then she made her way towards to the Goomart, where she had just been promoted from a Goo Spillage Human to a Very Important Unicorn shopping assistant, responsible for assisting all the VIUs with their goo needs. No matter how many times she saw the Goomart, she could never get over how brilliantly weird it was. It was the No. 1 goo shop in the UNIverse, and the oldest. The shelves were stocked to bursting with every magic goo you could imagine, and some that you couldn't. It was a treasure trove of slimy magic and Neon loved every inch of—

'OH, THANK HOOFS YOU'RE HERE, I HAVE A GOOMERGENCY!' came a cry that shattered her thoughts. A terrified looking Bronco Blazon, the new

Goo Spillage Cleaner, burst out of the Goomart and hid behind her.

'What is it now?' Neon groaned, just as a giant piece of gooey cheese came stomping out of the shop. It was wearing platform shoes.

'Oh no,' Neon said, taking a cautious step back.

The thing was huge, as tall as the Goomart itself. It smiled and wiggled with excitement, sending slobbery globs of cheese flying in all directions.

'BRONCO!' the cheese cooed. 'OH, BRONCO!'

'It's one of the Cheesy Feet goos,' Bronco explained at speed. 'You know, for fixing smelly feet. But it's gone off and morphed into ... *that*.'

Neon scratched her head. All magic in the UNIverse was done with goo – there was a goo for practically everything. But goo was unwieldy and when a goo went off, anything could happen.

'I COULDN'T BELIEVE MY CHEESE EYES WHEN I SAW YOU, BRONCO!' the cheese oozed. 'I JUST COULDN'T BELIEVE MY CHEESE EYES.'

'I think it's in love with me!' Bronco fretted. 'It's cheesy cheese.' He held up his goo wand, ready to pounce. Usually, most goos could be eliminated by a simple light touch of a goo wand, if you could get close enough.

'Ah, and it's wearing platform shoes because it was a product for feet,' Neon said. 'It all makes so much sense.'

'I HAVE BEAUTIFUL CHEESE FEET!'

'Save me,' Bronco pleaded, shakily handing Neon his goo wand.

'Pleasure,' Neon said with a smile, then without a second's pause she charged forwards, sliding right through the cheese's legs and expertly jabbing it in the shoe with the goo wand! Instantly, the whole thing went *POP*. Putrid cheese rained down on her until she was completely buried in the stuff! The stench was almost unbearable and Neon held her breath as she clawed her way out.

Bronco was crying with relief. 'That,' he said, 'was so cool!'

Neon proudly pulled the cheesy goo from her hair and flicked it on to the floor. Music started playing somewhere in the distance – it was the Mice Gurls' new single, 'Mice Up Your Life'.

'Just another day at the Goomart,' she said as she swaggered inside.

The owner of the Goomart, Old Lady Buck, greeted Neon with a nod and handed her a goo wand. Her long hair was pulled into a low ponytail and it swished behind her like a pony's as they walked to the VIU section. As soon as they got there, Neon spotted the blobs of goo dancing around the room, and the sound of applause. She caught a glimpse of a glittering red jumpsuit.

Old Lady Buck had used a decorating goo on the VIU department when she'd first built it many years ago. The goo had been called GUEST'S DREAM, so the colours and furniture and paintings would morph into the preferred style of the guest inside. Unfortunately, it had since gone off and now guests also experienced things they had literally dreamed of the night before. Sometimes it was wonderful things, like bunnies in meadows, and sometimes it was terrible, like a monster called Elgin who had fourteen eyes and burped up angry ants.

'Important day today, kid,' Old Lady Buck said, pushing her towards the room. 'You've got a VIU in need of holiday supplies and she's one tricky customer.'

'Neon!' came a cry, as Filly Spangle poked her head around the door. She glanced at Old Lady Buck, who was sneaking off down the aisle. 'Old Lady Buck! You're not helping too? I need expertise, not … no offence, Neon. She's *a human*.'

Filly Spangle and Neon had only recently become friends, after a rocky start. But Filly often said quite rude things, without really realising she was doing it.

'Bit harsh,' Neon said. 'I'm also a unicorn now, *remember*.' She turned and showed Filly her stripe of hair.

'Barely,' Filly said. 'I'm going to Lumino Falls, Neon. That requires some very important goos. For starters I need a specialised Lumino Falls sun cream, and I'll need a special Lumino Falls hair comb because the kelpies will do terrible things to me if I have the wrong one.'

'Kelpies?' Neon said, confused.

'Yeah, someone once dropped a jar of Scottish Legends goo into Lumino Falls and now there are millions of them. If you go swimming with the wrong comb, they get furious. I don't know why, it's just their thing.'

'So ... don't bring a comb?' Neon suggested.

'Oh, that's even worse. If you're comb-less, you can't pay the monster to borrow a goo canoe. It only accepts payment in combs.'

Neon blinked in bewilderment, then quietly whimpered, 'Old Lady Buck?'

'You've got this!' Old Lady Buck called over her shoulder, and Neon was sure she heard her chuckle.

'All right,' Neon said faintly. 'A comb, so you can go canoeing or whatever.'

Filly's face grew serious. 'You may mock me, Neon, but you would not be laughing if you saw what can happen if you bring the wrong comb to Lumino Falls.'

Sometimes, on particularly weird UNIverse days, Neon found her mind drifting back to the human world, where everything was normal and boring. Daytime in the UNIverse was night-time in the human world, and due to all the portal jumping, Neon never needed to sleep. It was now almost impossible for her to imagine what sleep felt like. She closed her eyes and pictured her parents tucked up in their bed, and the next-door neighbours – Priscilla and her mum, Mrs Knackerman … the whole town, sleeping soundly.

But Neon imagined *wrong* that day.

Priscilla wasn't tucked up in bed, and she certainly wasn't sleeping. She wasn't even at home.

She was at Neon's house.

2

Intruder in Neon's Room

A little earlier.

Priscilla heaved herself up and through Neon's
bedroom window and rolled across the room.

'Unicorns,' she said angrily under her breath. She
was too late! The portal had almost closed, only a tiny,
barely visible bit of the rip remained. Neon was already
in the UNIverse! *Again.*

'Every time,' she muttered. 'I can never catch her.'
Priscilla's plan was simple: catch Neon jumping
through the portal and snatch the portal opener from her
grasp. She'd been trying for *weeks*, but it was no good.
She'd even tried searching for it during the day when
Neon was working at Ratty's (her parents' weird cafe).
She decided Neon had to be keeping it on her at all times.

Priscilla could feel the fury growing inside her. Unicorn Hunters were born to sniff out unicorns and destroy their world. She was closer than any other UH had ever been. If she could just get hold of the lipstick, she'd be the most notorious and famous UH in the world. She could destroy THEM ALL!

Priscilla had one more plan to try.

She pulled one of her mother's old lipsticks from her bag.

'Time for a confusing switcheroo,' she said with a smirk. And she placed the lipstick in Neon's Ratty's apron pocket. If Neon kept the lipstick on her, then it must be in the apron pocket … She wore it all the time, it would be the perfect hiding place for it. Priscilla was hoping that *another* lipstick would cause her to leave the portal opener somewhere, thinking she was already carrying it. It might only work for a short while, especially as Neon's lipstick was green and all Priscilla could find was a bunch of red ones, but it would be enough time for Priscilla to get her hands on the portal opener.

But she had to be there, waiting. This plan required a SLEEPOVER.

Quietly, Priscilla crawled under Neon's bed.

And she waited.

3

Wrong Comb!

'NEON! I can't see anything on the label that says this *is* a Lumino Falls appropriate comb!'

'It *is*,' Neon lied. Truth be told, she had no idea, she just wanted to get Filly Spangle out of the shop.

They stood at the checkout glaring at each other. Neon lifted the goo pots out of the horse-shoe shaped shopping basket, clunking them on to the conveyer belt without taking her eyes off Filly.

'Intense shopping day?' Geldie O'Splendid said nervously as he scanned the pots at the till.

'Yes, if you must know,' Filly said, breaking eye contact and turning to Geldie while brandishing her VIU card. 'My parents let me use their VIU card so I could shop for my Lumino Falls holiday. I had a very important list, especially the comb I need to pay the goo canoe monster.'

'Oh,' Geldie said, holding up the comb, 'I don't think this is a—'

'THAT'S 400 GOLDS,' Neon said loudly, shooting Geldie a look.

Geldie put the comb in the shopping bag and then slowly handed the lot to Filly Spangle.

'You know,' he said, 'I'm also going to Lumino Falls for a holiday.'

'Not to Sprinkle Lodge Campgrounds, I'm sure,' Filly said with a chuckle.

'Oh yeah,' Geldie said. 'That's exactly where we're going – me and my dad.'

Geldie's dad was the famous Greg, the unicorn who had made up the horse-with-a-horn thing.

'Oh,' Filly said. 'Well, we should probably hang out. Maybe we can go swimming? I'm planning to do the dive to the Lumino Deeps. Maybe find some treasure'.

Geldie gulped. 'Sure. I love swimming with ancient, decaying goo monsters.'

'That's no way to speak about Filly!' Neon cried.

They both looked at her.

'The Lumino Deeps are full of ancient, out-of-date goo monsters,' Filly corrected her. 'Seriously, Neon, you call yourself a unicorn.' And with that, she marched out of the shop.

'You know that comb isn't the right one,' Geldie whispered.

'Does it really matter?' Neon asked.

Geldie nodded gravely.

'Ugh,' Neon said, handing Geldie her golds for the day. 'Buy her the right comb with these and try to swap it out when you see her.'

Geldie smiled.

'NEON!' came a cry, followed by the sound of galloping gooey hoofs. Neon looked up to see her best friend, Moya McGlow … riding … on a goo creature!

Moya was a big fan of Greg unicorns – you know, the made-up horses with horns – and she was always wearing head-to-toe Greg unicorn clothing. And now, much to Neon's disbelief, Moya was by some miracle riding an *actual* fake unicorn, made of goo.

'ISN'T IT AMAZING?!' she screeched, jiggling with excitement and making the unicorn wobble.

Neon only had to glance at it to know where it came from. She looked across the road to Whiskers & Gloop, the pet shop, and groaned.

HALF-PRICE MYSTERY MADE-UP PET GOOS read a hastily scribbled sign in the window.

A tiny child charged out on a gooey stegosaurus and immediately began crying with joy.

'Oh no,' Neon groaned.

'I GOT EXACTLY, EXACTLY, EXACTLY WHAT I WANTED!' Moya said, dismounting the horned horse and falling in a heap on the floor. It reared up and started kicking goo jars off the shelves before charging off.

'No!' Neon cried. 'This is beyond Bronco's clean-up abilities!'

Geldie grabbed the tannoy. 'Clean up on aisle one … and two … and three … nine, fourteen. CLEAN UP ON ALL THE AISLES, BRONCO!'

Bronco came racing out from the back room, saw what was happening and fainted.

'Oh dear boy,' Old Lady Buck said, pulling him to his feet. 'Playing dead will not stop the discount salads from eating you.'

'PONY!' Moya cried. 'COME BACK, PONY!' she turned back to Neon. 'I was waiting until I saw you to name him. Any ideas?'

'Menace!?' Neon said. 'Goo Smasher!?'

'Menace Goo Smasher!' Moya cheered. 'Oh I knew

you'd know exactly what would suit him!' And then she ran off screaming, 'MENACE GOO SMASHER, COME BACK!'

'Just another day –' Neon began as an escaped goo chicken flew into Geldie's face with a thud – 'at the Goomart.'

4

Twizzle

Moya and Menace Goo Smasher were waiting for Neon after she finished work.

'Jump on,' Moya insisted.

Awkwardly, Neon heaved herself up on to the gooey unicorn. It began to back up, making Neon wobble. Quickly, she started to sink into the goo, like she was going to fall right through to the ground!

'Can it take more than one rider?' Neon asked as she inched her way to the pavement.

'Hmm,' Moya said, producing a jar shaped like a unicorn head. 'Hang on …'

Neon watched with exasperation as Moya took her time inspecting the small print.

Soon, she was head-deep in the gooey bottom.

'… No. He cannot take more than one rider,' Moya

announced just as Neon hit the pavement with a *bang*. The unicorn's bottom *pinged* back into place.

'Cool!' a kid across the street cried, and immediately the owner of Whiskers & Gloop appeared beside him and thrust a tray of goos in his face.

'These pet goos are invincible,' he said. 'They are part of our UNREAL PETS THAT HUMANS BELIEVE IN collection. Would you like one?'

The little boy handed over some golds and picked a shimmering cube. He cracked it open and goo slowly seeped out. Neon watched the goo intently and seconds later a giant sea monster burst from it.

'LEAPING UNICORNS!' the pet shop owner shouted as he ducked for cover. 'You got the rarest one of all! That's the Kraken. Only a one in a billion chance of getting that sea monster.'

The boy turned pale and began trying to shove the goo back in the cube.

The monster rose higher, unfurling its gargantuan tentacles as it went.

'From Norway in the human world, I think,' the

owner said as he inched towards the shop door. 'Very famous,' he finished and bolted the door.

Neon gulped as the shadow of the gooey beast fell over them.

'It looks like ...' Neon began, the words failing her.

'A dragon in an octopus skirt,' Moya finished for her. 'Why are you looking at me like that? It does.'

The hulking beast hovered over the little boy, its single eye rolling around in its head. The poor boy was shaking so much he had begun to look blurry. The creature raised one giant tentacle high in the air ... and placed it gently on the boy's shoulder, giving him a reassuring pat.

'I LOVE HIM!' the boy said instantly, and Neon watched in amazement as he bounced off down the road, his monster floating above his head like a dreadful bunch of balloons.

Moya turned and cuddled into her unicorn's neck. 'I'M SO LUCKY I GOT MENACE GOO SMASHER! I LOVE YOU, MENACE GOO SMASHER!'

At that, Menace Goo Smasher charged forward and

smashed through the doors of Glittervoles cafe, sending customers flying.

'And he knew where to go!' Moya called back proudly to Neon. 'Menace Goo Smasher is *the best*.'

Suzette, the owner of Glittervoles, who Neon could never quite get over was a *squirrel* made of *sprinkles*, came rushing out.

'Who brought the goo Greg unicorn?' she cried.

Moya raised her hand nervously.

'Because he,' Suzette said breathlessly, 'IS FABULOUS!'

Suzette gave them the best table in Glittervoles, the one right by the window overlooking the town square. And because Moya had brought Menace Goo Smasher, they got free Volefizz drinks too.

Volefizz was the UNIverse's best drink. It tasted a little like strawberry lemonade warmed by sunshine and it came with a rodent in it. A vole, to be precise.

Neon nodded a hello to the rodent as it swirled in circles in her glass. Moya was too busy rifling through her bag to notice the drinks had arrived.

'Ah!' she said, holding a gooey magazine aloft. 'You're going to love this, Neon.'

THE GLOOPY

Lumino's No. 1 mag, where goo and style collide!

DRESS LIKE A HUMAN: NEON GALLUP STYLE INSPIRATION!

The Slimy Wardrobe has a special goo this month in honour of the UNIverse's newest unicorn from the world of humans, or as we like to call her, a humicorn. This humicorn has some serious style – teaming tie-dye tights with jelly shoes and a slouchy dress, she always looks effortlessly humicorny! Get the Slimy Wardrobe Neon Gallup HUMICORN goo half price with this coupon.

'Humicorn?' Neon cried, grabbing the magazine and checking she hadn't read it wrong. 'No, they did refer to me as a humicorn – FOUR times.'

Moya inspected the magazine. 'Actually, one time they referred to you as "humicorny". Quite cool there's a Slimy Wardrobe goo of your outfit, don't you think?'

'Not if they call it a humicorn outfit,' Neon said, crossing her arms in proud annoyance.

'Food's on me today, ladies. And I've got your favourite …' Suzette said, plonking down a large platter of tiny glittery chunks. 'The Glitter Chunk Platter!'

Neon and Moya smiled weakly. Suzette was always trying to push the Glitter Chunk Platter on customers, even though it was by far the worst thing on the menu.

'I was actually going to order a sparkle burger,' Moya said quietly. But when she saw Suzette's raised sprinkle eyebrow, she added, 'But now that I see this Glitter Chunk Platter it's … ALL I WANT.'

'Mmm,' Neon said, taking one of the chunks and plopping it on her tongue. 'So glittery, so … chunky.'

She rolled it about in her mouth and felt the glitter

coating her tongue. It was like eating a glob of goo covered in sand. It was exactly how she would've imagined a chunk of glitter would taste.

Neon felt Suzette's eager eyes on her as she gulped it down and tried not to gag.

'Well?' Suzette asked.

'Mmm,' Neon managed. 'Mmm.'

'Oh,' Suzette said. 'Before I forget, this letter came for you, Neon.'

'Letter?' Neon said. 'Who would send me post – and why would they send it to Glittervoles?'

Suzette shrugged. 'Maybe because you're always here.' She dropped the envelope on the table before bounding off, shedding some sprinkles as she went.

Neon quickly plucked the envelope from the table and inspected it. It was green and glossy and a small glob of slime sealed it shut.

'Open it!' Moya said, fishing a chewed Glitter Chunk from her mouth and placing it back on the platter with a look of disgust.

But the second Neon opened the letter, she saw that

it wasn't a letter at all. There was nothing inside but a splodge of green goo.

'Strange,' Neon said.

Moya gasped. 'Strange Goo Society!'

Neon's eyes widened. She had found the Strange Goo Society once before. They were a mysterious unicorn club whose members secretly brewed the most unusual of goos.

'I doubt they would be sending me a letter,' Neon

said. 'The last time I was there I triggered an emergency evacuation by opening a transportation goo. I've never been allowed back.'

'Even so, that's definitely the Strange Goo Society,' Moya said. 'They send blank letters and if you're a true member you know exactly what to do with it.'

Neon's first instinct was to try to eat the letter, but she knew that was almost certainly wrong.

Moya pushed the Glitter Chunk Platter aside and leaned forward eagerly, resting her chin in her hands. 'So … activate the letter. Maybe it's important.'

'I don't know how,' Neon said. She plucked the glob of goo off the envelope and stretched it between her fingers. 'I don't know what I'm doing.'

'I bet you do and you don't even realise it,' Moya said encouragingly as Neon dropped the goo on to the table with a defeated *splat*.

The second she did though, she noticed something in the glob of goo – a tiny flicker of impossible light deep inside it.

At the sight of it, Menace Goo Smasher reared up and charged off around the room.

'I forgot he was here,' Moya said, leaping to her feet and chasing after him. 'MENACE GOO SMASHER! WE'VE NOT FINISHED DINING YET!'

The gooey unicorn was pelting into diners and sending food and drinks flying. There were screams and shrieks and smashes, but to Neon it was all a distant hum. It was as if she was melting away to somewhere else. The light inside the glob of goo glowed brighter, then the whole table became sloppy. Her hands began to tingle and slip through it. She looked around nervously, but everyone was too busy wrestling the gooey unicorn to notice. The letter, meanwhile, was suspended in the goo, folding itself into the shape of a slide that went straight through the floor.

'Bit weird,' Neon said, tapping the slide with her jelly shoe. The slide wobbled. Her shoe was stuck! She wiggled her leg, but that made things worse. She felt a pull, and down she slipped, under the goo and away to somewhere else.

'Filly?' Neon said in astonishment as she got to her feet. Her friend was standing over her, dressed like a chef and wearing a tall rainbow-striped hat. All around them were workstations, complete with different goos and decorations neatly arranged in little bowls. And it wasn't just them. There were around twenty unicorns in the room, all dressed like chefs too.

'I thought you'd like to come to a brewing class,' Filly said. 'This one is *very* important. It's a thank you for helping me find the right holiday supplies, and especially the right comb so I don't get attacked by kelpies.'

'About that—' Neon said quietly, but Filly cut her off.

'I convinced the Strange Goo Society to have you back.'

'Wait, this is a Strange Goo Society thing?' Neon said.

'*Obviously*,' Filly replied. 'You just slid through some goo from a letter to get here. Now get your apron on.'

'Oh,' Neon said, glancing up at the ceiling as she searched for an exit. 'I was actually with Moya in Glittervoles and it feels rude leaving her. Menace Goo

Smasher was in full Menace Goo Smasher mode when I left.'

Filly shuddered. 'I *told* her to call him Pearl or Trotty Wonder, but she doesn't listen to me.'

'I like Trotty Wonder,' Neon said with an amused smile.

'You've got to give them proper names,' Filly said seriously. 'Menace Goo Smasher is *not* a proper name. Trotty Wonder sounds much more serious.'

Neon pulled a chef's hat over her face to stop herself from laughing.

'It just sits on top of your head,' Filly said, hoisting it up for her.

Suddenly, a voice boomed, 'WELCOME! You are about to embark on the ultimate hour of goo brewing!'

Drops of goo began to fall fast from the ceiling, like really enthusiastic rain.

Neon ducked as goo droplets splatted to the ground in a chorus of squelches. She scanned the room for the owner of the voice, but the goo was getting thicker. It seemed to be sticking to her face. In mere seconds,

36

she couldn't see anything at all.

'Filly, what is happening?' she hissed.

'I don't talk during goo brewing classes,' Filly hissed back. 'They require my full attention.'

'Now spatula that goo off your face and get it in the pan!' the voice boomed.

Neon frantically felt around for the spatula she had seen at her workstation. Her fingers slipped over goo and finally hit something. 'The spatula!' she cheered as she lifted it in the air triumphantly and began peeling the goo off her face.

As the room slowly came back into focus, she could see Filly hard at work, already slopping the goo from her face into a pan. And she could see the owner of the voice.

'Who IS *THAT*?' Neon whispered, staring up at the tall unicorn with actual sparkly skin and a corkscrew moustache that twirled all the way to the floor. 'Because that moustache is not sanitary! I hope these aren't edible goos – they'll have hair in them! He should tie his moustache up!'

Neon had recently done a Goo Health and Safety

course at the Goomart with Old Lady Buck and she had learned three important things:

1. Much like any other food prep, you should tie your hair up when making food goos.
2. Always wash your hands.
3. Never EVER try to negotiate with talking cheeses.

'Neon,' Filly snapped. 'That right there is Twizzle, the most famous unicorn chef in the UNIverse and the most celebrated member of the Strange Goo Society. He's travelled all over the UNIverse – he's seen bits no other unicorn has seen, scaled heights no other unicorn has scaled, dived to depths no other unicorn has dived!'

'Why ... if he's a chef?' Neon said.

Filly sighed impatiently. 'For goo ingredients, of course. He discovers new and weird things from across the UNIverse. They inspire his goos.'

'You mean there's weirder things than a talking squirrel made of sprinkles who owns a restaurant?'

'That's not a weird thing,' Filly said flatly.

'Why is his skin glittery?' Neon whispered.

Filly rolled her eyes. 'Obviously he's recently been swimming in Lumino Falls. I'm going to be so sparkly after my holiday there.'

'Now, take the sprinkle powder and add it to the goo,' Twizzle said with a nod.

Neon chucked the whole pot of sprinkle powder in and turned back to Filly to continue their conversation.

'But only add a little, or else,' Twizzle warned, 'you will find that it—'

BANG!

Instantly, Neon felt her feet leave the floor and she tumbled backwards into the workstation behind her. The goo from that workstation went flying through the air, Filly batted it with her pan, sending it hurtling forward, and it landed with a *squelch* on Neon's head.

The whole room watched in silence as Neon peeled strands of goo out of her hair. Then Twizzle was looming over her, a slight smile curling beneath his ridiculous moustache.

'Apologies!' Neon said sheepishly. 'I'm quite new.

Half human – I live in that world half the time, and I'm prone to making mistakes.' She heard Filly groan with embarrassment behind her. She extended a hand. 'I'm Neon. Neon Gallup.'

Twizzle stared at her, blinking in bewilderment. 'Well, Neon,' he said eventually, 'I hope you like my moustache.'

'Um, it's definitely *a look*.'

'Because you're about to grow a lot of them.'

'What?!' Neon cried, and instantly her upper lip began getting hot. Coils of hair sprang from her skin, *pinging* up and hitting her on the forehead.

She turned desperately to Filly, who didn't seem to know whether to die of embarrassment or die laughing.

'This is the very simple Twizzle Moustache goo,' Twizzle explained to the group. 'Now, as you can see, it's fast-acting. And Neon will be delighted to hear it is also long-lasting.'

Neon caught a glimpse of herself in the window – she had about fifteen moustaches now! All moulding into one mega, and very heavy, moustache.

She began to tip forward with the weight of it.

'I think you rather suit it,' Twizzle said.

Neon pulled her goo wand from her back pocket and began swatting it. Just one hit of the goo wand could get rid of anything – sentient cheeses in platform shoes, absolutely anything! But not this moustache. It kept growing back.

'Much easier just to shave it,' Twizzle said. 'It's a special goo I brew, unofficial, can't be sold at the Goomart because a goo wand won't get rid of it! Now, everyone bottle your brew and let's take a break and clean the kitchen. I have a surprise for you, something I found far away in a hidden corner of Mystica.'

Everyone apart from Neon gasped.

'What's Mystica?' Neon whispered to Filly.

Filly grinned. 'It's the most mysterious city in the UNIverse.'

'Without further ado,' Twizzle said, 'I present to the Strange Goo Society a secret never to be spoken of outside these walls … THE TROTTING SWEET SHOP OF MYSTICA!'

5

The Trotting Sweet Shop
of Mystica

'And *then*,' Neon said, leaping from Moya's bed and holding her arms wide for effect, 'a sweet shop, mounted on four HORSE legs, came trotting into the room and neighed.'

Moya's mouth fell open. 'No way!'

'Way!' Neon said.

'Hang on,' Geldie said. 'You just told us that Twizzle said it was a secret never to be spoken of. I don't think you were meant to tell us. We're not in the Strange Goo Society.'

'Hmm,' Neon said, plonking herself back down on the bed. 'So *you* keep it a secret and then it's fine?'

Geldie put his head in his hands and sighed loudly.

'It was so cool,' Neon went on. 'Oh, but not the moustache bit. Luckily, Twizzle knew the recipe for a really good barber goo and now all my moustaches have disappeared.'

Geldie and Moya looked confused.

'Anyway!' Neon said. 'Twizzle said in Mystica all the shops can trot, and when you eat a sweet it shows you a secret the UNIverse is keeping. But we weren't allowed to touch them.'

Moya and Geldie breathed a sigh of relief.

'I thought you were going to say you'd sneaked us some to eat!' Geldie said, shaking his head. 'I don't fancy messing with magic from weird parts of the UNIverse.'

Moya shook her head too, from where she was sitting atop Menace Goo Smasher.

'Oh yeah,' Neon said. 'I didn't sneak any for you to

eat … but I did pick this one up off the floor and I thought I might try it!'

She held up a glowing orange sweet.

'Oh no,' Geldie whimpered. 'Neon, it's not a good idea. I bet you weren't meant to take that.'

'What harm can it do?' Neon said. 'It'll just tell me a secret about the UNIverse. It would be nice to know something that none of the other unicorns know! Everyone knows more about the UNIverse than me.'

And with that, she popped it in her mouth.

Tellingly, Menace Goo Smasher began shaking like a plated jelly.

Moya dived on to the bed and Geldie got to his feet.

'How do you feel?' he said as Neon gulped the sweet down.

Neon slumped.

'She's dead!' Moya cried.

'It's just pure dead disappointment,' Neon said. 'I don't feel anything!'

'What a relief,' Geldie said.

Moya made her way to the door. 'Come on, I think

45

we have some Neigh Whip cones in the freezer.'

'Oooh,' Neon said. She loved the Neigh Whip cones, they were like ice cream cones only they made you neigh every time you licked them.

She stood up to follow the others, and that was when she saw it. Sitting right there on Moya's pile of washing.

'Why are you looking at me like that?' it said.

'Can … can … you … see it?' Neon shrieked, pointing nervously in its direction.

'My washing pile?' Moya said. 'Yes, it's massive. I haven't washed any clothes for three weeks!'

'No,' Neon said. 'On top of the washing pile!'

'Huh?' Moya and Geldie said together.

'They can't see me,' the thing said. 'And if you try to describe me they'll only laugh.'

'It's … a … it's got a little fairy face, and the body of a … horse—'

'More of a pony,' the thing corrected her.

'And it's wearing jelly shoes.'

Moya and Geldie laughed.

'Told you,' the little thing said. 'Tell them more about the shoes.'

'No, seriously,' Neon said. 'It's there and it has shoes, four of them, and they are glowing and flashing. And it has a hat.'

'Tell them about the hat,' the thing said eagerly.

'OK, I'm worried,' Geldie said.

'It's a Mice Gurls bucket hat,' Neon said. 'It says MICE GURLS ARE THE SQUEAKIEST in a heart that looks like cheese.'

The thing took off its hat to reveal a unicorn horn.

'And it has a horse-with-a-horn kind of unicorn horn!' Neon yelled, pointing madly at it.

Moya narrowed her eyes at the washing pile. 'I think … there might be something wrong with you, Neon …'

Geldie gasped. 'No, it must be the sweet! It's working! It's the secret!'

'You're from Mystica?' Neon said. 'Are you what creatures look like in Mystica?'

The little thing looked confused. 'No, I was made by a sweet company for their magic sweets. You don't seriously believe things like me exist?' It laughed. 'What are you, *a human*?'

'I am actually. And a unicorn.'

The thing looked confused again.

'Never mind, never mind,' Neon said, inching closer. 'You're meant to show me a secret the UNIverse is keeping.'

'You're not allowed to tell them,' the thing said, nodding to Moya and Geldie.

'What's it saying?' Moya asked, crawling towards the pile of clothes.

'We don't want to know,' Geldie said nervously.

'Pinkie promise I won't tell,' Neon said to the little thing, holding out a pinkie but crossing her fingers behind her back.

48

'I only have hoofs,' the thing said.

Neon cupped her hand so it was horse-shoe shaped. 'Hoovie promise,' she said, holding her hand out.

'WHAT IS GOING ON?!' Geldie cried.

The little thing leaned in closer and lifted off its hat again, only this time its unicorn horn began to glow, casting words across the walls.

THE LEGEND OF THE LONG-LOST UNICORN HUNTER

Neon shivered. The thought of Unicorn Hunters made her uneasy – she had too many of them to deal with in Brunty. She came to the UNIverse to escape Unicorn Hunters!

'This is a secret the UNIverse keeps,' the little thing said.

What does it mean? Neon thought, reading the strange words splattered across the walls.

'Oh, has the thing moved?' Moya said, scurrying around the room.

49

'No,' Neon said quietly as she read. 'There's something else here.'

'Don't tell!' the little thing said.

*THE LONG-LOST UNICORN HUNTER LIVES
HERE STILL … IN THE UNIverse.*

*THE LONG-LOST UNICORN HUNTER IS
AMONG US.*

*THEY CAN BE FOUND BENEATH THE GOO.
BUT THEY DON'T HIDE IN THE SHADOWS,
THEY ARE KNOWN, THEY ARE SEEN.*

'Tell us,' Moya said. 'What's on the wall?'

Neon gulped. 'It's … nothing,' she said. 'It's nothing.'

But it wasn't nothing, and Neon knew it.

And with that, the strange little thing disappeared in a *ploof* of sherbet.

'Sherbet!' Moya cried. 'I can see that!'

6

What Lurks Under the Bed

Neon took out her lipstick and drew a line across Moya's bedroom wall. Soon the portal began to fizz and crack and tear open.

'Are you sure you're all right?' Moya asked.

'Absolutely,' Neon said, forcing a smile. And with that, she dived into the human world.

Back in her bedroom, it was morning and she did as she always did – she took off her Goomart apron and pulled on her Ratty's one. But something was different – it felt heavier than normal. She felt the front pocket and was surprised to find—

'A lipstick,' she said out loud. 'What's that doing here?'

She popped the lid off. Red lipstick.

'Mum! Dad!' she called. 'Did you put a lipstick in my Ratty's apron pocket?'

'Did you put some socks in the toaster?' her dad called back.

'WHAT?' Neon said.

'Oh,' her dad said, appearing in the doorway. 'I thought we were playing a silly game, but you have *actually* found a lipstick.' He spotted her other one, the *magic* portal-opening one on the floor. 'You've found TWO lipsticks.'

'Not that one,' Neon said quickly. 'It's … nothing … just … ignore it.' She kicked it away, under her bed.

Neon's mum popped her head around the door. 'What's this about lipsticks in aprons and socks in toasters?'

'Did you put this in my apron pocket?' Neon asked, brandishing the red lipstick.

'No,' her mum said. 'I've never seen that lipstick before. It's not mine, I prefer more unpredictable colours.'

Neon's dad smiled at her mother. 'And that is why you are the world's best artist,' he said.

'Oh stop it!' she said bashfully.

Neon felt the blood drain from her face. If they hadn't put the lipstick in her pocket, then … She ran to the window and stared out at the town. In the distance some UHs were digging holes, looking for the portal opener. That's all they ever did. They'd been doing it since the first day she arrived in Brunty and they hadn't stopped since. They knew it was somewhere nearby, but they didn't know where and they didn't know what it looked like. But if someone had planted a lipstick in Neon's apron then they were clearly sending her a message.

They knew what the portal opener looked like … and they knew she had it!

While talk of lipsticks in aprons and socks in toasters was going on above the bed, Priscilla was wedged underneath it, trying desperately not to squeal with glee.

The plan hadn't gone to plan at all. She had hoped by putting another lipstick in Neon's pocket she might mistake it for her portal opener, leaving the real one in the room for Priscilla to swipe. After all, it must be hard being organised and keeping track of things when you lead a secret double life.

Instead, Neon had discovered the lipstick instantly and Priscilla had momentarily thought the plan was thwarted, but it actually worked brilliantly because Neon had kicked the portal opener out of sight of her parents, and straight into Priscilla's face!

As the confusion unfolded above her, Priscilla popped the lid off the lipstick, her face illuminated by the magical green glow. Immediately her eyes flashed red. She could feel the fury of a thousand Unicorn Hunters coursing through her veins. Every UH in the world dreamed of finding the portal opener and fulfilling their destiny of wiping out every last unicorn on the planet! She wanted more than anything to grab it and dive through the portal and DESTROY EVERYTHING!

'Right, come on, Neon, the cafe's getting busy,' Mrs Gallup said. 'We could do with some help on the coffee machine.'

'Those ratpuccinos won't make themselves!' Mr Gallup joked. 'And don't worry about that lipstick. I'm sure there's a perfectly logical explanation.'

'Hmm,' Neon said, and much to Priscilla's delight they all marched out of the room.

'The long-lost portal opener,' Priscilla breathed. 'It's mine. IT'S FINALLY MINE!'

7

A Very Unfortunate Ratty's Makeover

After she had served the line of waiting Ratty's customers with ratpuccinos, Neon busied herself tucking in chairs and propping up the cafe's signature giant cuddly toy rats.

All she could think about was the other lipstick. What did it mean? Was it a threat? Who knew her secret? She wished Alaric was there to help. He was a giant ghost rat from the UNIverse who had made Ratty's cafe his home, and he could always be counted on in a sticky spot. But he was on holiday, in Space, and completely uncontactable.

In the corner of the cafe, a group of UHs were talking loudly. Priscilla's mum, Patricia Knackerman, was there, commanding the proceedings.

'I want everything to be perfect,' Neon could hear her saying. 'His arrival is the biggest thing to happen to our group. He says the time has almost come when we will open the portal – he says he can smell it!'

They all cackled.

Neon edged closer to hear more.

'He's due imminently. Oh, Douglas, you're wearing the wrong T-shirt! We're wearing the tie-dye ones now, not the old 1970s flower power ones.'

'Sorry,' Douglas muttered, turning red.

'We must look our best. We're the biggest group of UHs on the planet, in the hottest portal opener spot in the world,' Mrs Knackerman prattled on. 'Every UH knows it's here. Quite frankly, it's beginning to look bad we haven't found it yet.'

'Yes,' came a gruff voice. 'It is.'

Mrs Knackerman began to choke. 'Your greatness,' she said. Then she got up and performed a deeply awkward bow.

Neon turned to see a man, tall and lean with golden hair and red-flecked eyes, standing in the doorway. He wore a green cloak embroidered with frowning unicorns and his nails were as long as bear claws. Just the sight of him made her shiver.

He began to sniff. 'Yes,' he said. 'I can smell the unicorns already.'

Neon started to back away.

'NEON!' Mrs Knackerman cried, making Neon jump so violently she practically fell over.

'Your finest ratpuccino for Mr Ragwort, please.'

The man set his gaze on Neon and glared at her. His stare felt like hot burning poison sliding down her throat and scorching her belly.

'Coming right up,' Neon managed with a gulp.

She began racing towards the counter, but then Mrs Knackerman said something that made her screech to a halt.

'Priscilla – why are you holding a GREEN LIPSTICK high in the air like that?'

Neon felt her stomach hit the floor. Slowly, she turned, hoping it wasn't her lipstick. Anything but that. But there it was.

Priscilla was staring through her like a zombie, the battered green lipstick firmly in her fist. How had she got hold of it?

'I found the portal opener,' Priscilla said eerily, not taking her eyes off Neon.

'What?' Mrs Knackerman said, looking awkwardly from her daughter to Mr Ragwort and back again.

Neon inched forward, her mind moving at a million miles per hour and her feet barely moving at all.

Mr Ragwort got to Priscilla first.

'Hmm,' he said, taking the lipstick.

Neon could feel the sweat dripping down her fore-head. This was it! The day she destroyed the UNIverse and all her friends!

She watched helplessly as Mr Ragwort sniffed the lipstick.

She squeezed her eyes shut. This was it!

Then all of a sudden, Mr Ragwort erupted into a hysterical laugh. 'No, this isn't it!' he said with a snort.

'WHAT?' Neon cried.

'It's not the portal opener,' Mr Ragwort said. 'The girl is clearly lying. Or a complete idiot.'

'WHAT?' Neon cried again before she could stop herself. 'I mean … I just … wow,' she stopped, noticing Mrs Knackerman had fixed her with a suspicious stare. 'That's *such* a shame for you all, because you all … dig so much …'

'It *is* the portal opener,' Priscilla insisted. 'I've even seen it being used.'

Mr Ragwort laughed again. 'Dear girl, I know my unicorns and they wouldn't make a portal opener out of something so silly! These are THE MOST POWERFUL BEINGS ON THE PLANET, they would never make a lipstick a magical item – who would do that?!'

Neon tried not to smile. Then she thought of the portal opener Moya had, which was a box of chocolate snowballs, and arguably even sillier. Mr Ragwort didn't know *anything* about unicorns.

'But it *is* the portal opener!' Priscilla wailed. 'It is! It is! It is!'

'Priscilla,' Mrs Knackerman snapped. 'That's

enough, you're embarrassing yourself.'

'I'll show you!' Priscilla cried. And much to Neon's horror, she snatched the lipstick back from Mr Ragwort and popped off the lid.

The problem was, Priscilla hadn't actually seen Neon activate the portal opener, which meant she made the wrong assumption about using it. Instead of using the lipstick to draw a simple line across the cafe wall, Priscilla smeared it across her lips!

Neon froze and suddenly she felt very sick. Was Priscilla's face going to crack open? Would a tidal wave of stars and glitter ooze out? Would the inside of Priscilla's head reveal the UNIverse?! How gory was it going to get?!

The room fell quiet.

Neon rushed over to Priscilla and prodded her bottom lip.

'I'm so sorry about this, Mr Ragwort, your greatness,' Mrs Knackerman said.

Nothing was happening.

'Why is NOTHING HAPPENING?' Priscilla growled at Neon.

Mrs Knackerman couldn't take any more. She jumped up from her chair and marched across the room. 'Priscilla, *please*. Sit down.'

'Why don't you believe me?' Priscilla cried. 'I've discovered the biggest secret in the whole world, and you don't believe me!'

In all the commotion, Neon took her chance. She slid the green lipstick from Priscilla's grasp.

'That's mine!' Priscilla growled, snatching it back – only Neon had been quick and swapped it for the red lipstick. She hastily tucked the portal opener into her apron pocket and made for the door.

'Hang on *just* a minute, Neon Gallup!' Mrs Knackerman shouted. Neon froze.

'Yes?' she squeaked. Every inch of her was wobbling like Menace Goo Smasher. Slowly she turned to face her fate.

'You haven't made Mr Ragwort's ratpuccino!' Mrs Knackerman cried.

Neon practically collapsed with relief. 'Coming right up,' she said quickly, trying to hold herself together.

'Stop being so silly, Priscilla,' Neon could hear Mrs Knackerman hissing at her daughter. 'He's the most knowledgable UH in the world, my darling. Please don't do anything like that again. He's going to help us find the portal opener. We're so close.'

'A child isn't going to find the portal opener – I am!' Mr Ragwort laughed. 'And anyway, don't you remember the legend of the Long-Lost Unicorn Hunter? We've got help on the inside, so we might not even need a portal opener.'

The cup Neon was holding slipped from her grasp and smashed on the floor.

The Long-Lost Unicorn Hunter is among us. She saw the words again in her head.

Everyone looked at her.

She couldn't stop her hands from shaking. The Long-Lost Unicorn Hunter – like the trotting sweet shop of Mystica sweet had said!

'Hurry up with my ratpuccino!' Mr Ragwort shouted. 'And you,' he said, sneering at Priscilla. 'I don't need silly little children with their silly little lies

distracting me from my mission.'

Neon frowned as she poured the ratpuccino. Even if Priscilla *was* trying to destroy the UNIverse, she still felt sorry for her.

That night, Neon put the lipstick back in its hiding place in the window sill, where she had first found it. It had been safe there for a long time before Neon arrived in Brunty, and it would be safe for a long time more. She wiped a tear from her cheek as she closed the lid and made a very grown-up promise to herself, that for the sake of the UNIverse and those who she loved in it, she would never ever use the lipstick again.

8

The Science of Portals and a Gooey Guest

That night, Neon couldn't sleep. She lay in bed watching the globs of goo bounce about in her lava lamp, wondering if there would ever be a time when the Unicorn Hunters gave up trying to destroy the UNIverse. Or if they would at least move out of Brunty. That would be *really* nice.

What if one day they believed Priscilla? What if Priscilla found the lipstick again? What if Priscilla told them that Neon was a unicorn? Why hadn't Priscilla mentioned that, actually? And what about the Unicorn Hunter from her Mystica sweet – there was one already in the UNIverse, lying in wait and Mr Ragwort knew it! Mr Ragwort was probably so confident he'd get to the UNIverse because there was an UH on the inside who could open a portal for him!

Neon leaped out of bed. While staying away from the UNIverse was undoubtedly the best thing, maybe telling everyone the secret about the Long-Lost Unicorn Hunter hiding inside it was … bester?

She ran to the window sill to fetch the lipstick from its hiding place, but before she got there an almighty *BANG* sounded.

Glitter rained down and pooled at her ankles. She looked up and was surprised to see a portal had opened above her.

'There you are!' came a familiar voice.

'Moya!' Neon said with relief – for a second she had worried it might be the Long-Lost Unicorn Hunter.

'Where have you been?' Moya asked as she munched on a chocolate snowball. 'Bronco smashed some Roller-skating Vampire goos and can't clean them up! It's like the most dangerous roller-skating rink ever in there!'

Moya's face hovered above her, but her portal was getting bigger.

'Uh, Moya …' Neon said, as she watched the portal

spread so wide it was too big to contain Moya and she fell to the floor with a thud. When she stood up, her hair was still in the portal.

'That'll keep the portal open,' Moya said. 'So glad I sculpted my hair in a unicorn horn shape today. Now, tell me, what's going on? Why aren't you in the Goomart?'

Neon didn't waste any time. She told her about Priscilla finding the lipstick and knowing the secret, about Mr Ragwort and how close she had come to destroying the UNIverse. And about the fact that Brunty was ninety-nine per cent UNICORN HUNTERS.

'But the lipstick didn't work on Priscilla!' Neon finished. 'Which is a relief.'

Moya nodded. 'Of course it wouldn't open on a living thing, that would be gross!'

Neon laughed. 'Something finally went my way!'

'But it will open a portal,' Moya said through munches of chocolate snowball.

'What?' Neon cried. 'How?'

'When she wipes it off. Every portal opener contains traces of magic goo and when she wipes the lipstick off it'll transfer to a tissue, and tissues aren't living things, so …'

'No!' Neon cried, racing to her window. Across the wall, she could see blazing light coming from Priscilla's bathroom. Stars *pinged* across the grass.

'Oh no, oh no, no, no,' Neon fretted.

There was another thud.

'MENACE GOO SMASHER!' Moya cheered. 'Welcome to the human world.'

The portal had grown big enough for the crazy animal to land in Neon's room too …

'WHAT?!' Neon cried, whipping round to see. The big gooey menace nudged Moya with his muzzle, knocking her over … and her portal closed.

'Great,' Neon said flatly. 'I have a portal to the UNIverse next door and a GIANT GOOEY UNICORN IN MY BEDROOM.'

At that, Menace Goo Smasher took offence. He pointed his nose haughtily in the air and jumped out of the window.

'He's in your garden now,' Moya said. 'Oh no, he's jumped the wall and is now in your neighbour's garden.'

Neon watched in horror as Menace Goo Smasher sampled some of the Knackermans' tulips.

'Ooh this is bad,' she fretted. '*Really* bad.'

'The portal at the Knackermans will close, once someone jumps through,' Moya said. 'Well, once the person *who opened it* jumps through.'

'Well, that was me, wasn't it? Because it was my lipstick that did it,' Neon asked hopefully, even though she *knew* she was wrong.

Moya frowned. 'But you said Priscilla used the lipstick, so technically *she* opened the portal. She'll have to jump through it to the UNIverse to close it. Sorry, I can see by your face that was not what you wanted to hear.'

Neon chewed her nails and thought hard, as out beyond the window Menace Goo Smasher swished his gooey mane and trotted around in excited circles, churning up the Knackermans' lawn.

'So you're telling me the only option we have is to get Priscilla through the portal to close it? And then we'll somehow have to return her to the human world, without her seeing a thing?!'

Moya nodded.

'You want me to take her to the UNIverse and back *without her noticing*?' Neon cried.

'Luckily, it's night-time, so if she's sleeping and you make sure not to wake her, then it should be easy!' Moya said.

'Sure,' Neon said with a groan. 'That sounds so easy.'

'Easy-peasy unicorn squeezy!' Moya cheered, holding up her hand for a high five.

'I was being sarcastic,' Neon said. 'It sounds impossible.'

'We can do it,' Moya said. 'I'll get Menace Goo Smasher, you get Priscilla,' then she turned and yelled, 'MENACE GOO SMASHER! COME HERE RIGHT NOW!'

'Quietly!' Neon pleaded. 'Deal with it QUIETLY.'

'Oh,' Moya said. 'That'll be harder.'

Neon watched as more waves of glitter escaped the Knackermans' bathroom and spilt on to the grass. She couldn't waste a second more – she grabbed her lipstick from its hiding place and flung herself out of the window. She landed with an uncomfortable rustle in the hedge below.

'I might use the stairs and then the human door,' Moya whispered down to her.

Neon scuttled across the grass and over the wall, jumping from bush to clump of flowers. She gave Menace Goo Smasher a glare as she went. But when she'd made it to the Knackermans' cottage, she came to a screeching halt when she saw what was inside the spare room window.

'Mr Ragwort,' she whimpered. He was sleeping in the Knackermans' house!

She started to shake. If Mr Ragwort saw this! *Any* of this!

'I'll give you a leg up,' Moya said. Neon saw with relief that her other hand was firmly clutching Menace Goo Smasher's mane. With her free hand, Moya heaved

Neon in through the bathroom window.

'Get back to the UNIverse,' Neon whispered down to her. 'That's Mr Ragwort in their spare room. All the UHs worship him, they say he's the best UH in the world. Though I have my suspicions.'

Moya peered in the window with interest while Menace Goo Smasher *smooshed* his muzzle on the glass, sliming all over it.

'It's almost funny, isn't it?' Moya said. 'A portal's opened right next to him, and there's a goo unicorn and two other actual unicorns watching him sleep and he hasn't even woken up. I can't be sure, but I'm almost convinced he's *not* the best UH in the world.'

Another burst of glitter shot towards Neon, practically knocking her off her feet.

'This is getting out of hand,' she said as she scanned the room. The portal wasn't hard to find – the bin had become a swirling vortex about the size of a car. She ran to Priscilla's bed and slowly started inching the bed frame towards the portal.

Priscilla snored and stirred. A star *pinged* off her

forehead. Neon ducked behind the bed!

Priscilla snored again.

Neon whimpered. She inched the bed closer and closer to the portal, until finally they were through! They slipped into sparkling Lumino. The sun was green that day and Neon quickly pulled the bedcovers over Priscilla's face so the glare wouldn't wake her.

Moya and Menace Goo Smasher trotted up to her just as the portal closed.

'See,' Moya whispered. 'It was easy. Now take her home and then come back for a Volefizz.'

Priscilla snored again.

Neon brandished her lipstick and drew a line across a nearby wall, and soon the portal fizzed open. Gently, Neon pushed the bed back through to the human world and the portal closed behind her.

That'll do, she thought, deciding to leave Priscilla and her bed in the middle of the room. It was too risky pushing her any further. She had to get out! She ran to Priscilla's bathroom and closed the door behind her. *Pull yourself together, Neon*, she told herself. She splashed some water on her face, then took out the lipstick. Her hands were shaking! She dropped it with a *clang* in the sink! It swirled around with the draining water.

'Ugh,' Neon whispered, shaking the water off. Then she drew a line across the mirror and the portal fizzed open.

She dived through head first.

But it felt a little different this time.

A little bumpier.

She fell for longer and it was darker.

She eventually landed ... with an unexpected *splash*.

9

A Comb for a Goo Canoe

Neon kicked up through liquid goo and broke the surface, coughing and gasping for air. It was immediately obvious she wasn't in Lumino. All around her, gooey waterfalls cascaded into the pool she had fallen into. Cliffs peppered with candyfloss-pink trees rose up high around her and glinted in the bright green sun.

She felt something tug her leg and she looked down. Beneath the surface of the goo thousands of eyes were looking up at her.

'Oh no,' she whispered. 'The water in the sink must've messed with the portal opener when I dropped it!'

'NO COMB!' came a shout.

'Uh-oh,' Neon said, because she knew where she

was. 'I'm in Lumino Falls and I don't have a comb.'

A kelpie broke the surface. She was a monster with a gloopy face and wild luminous eyes the size of apples. She looked furious.

'Hellllo,' Neon said awkwardly. 'I realise I don't have a comb, but if I'd known I was coming, I definitely would've brought one.'

The kelpie hissed and threw some goo in Neon's hair.

Another kelpie popped out from the watery goo. Then another and another and another.

'I'm going to die,' Neon whimpered. She pulled out her lipstick and tried to draw across the goo. But the portal just fizzled and closed. Her portal opener was well and truly ruined!

Just then, someone broke through the waterfall in a goo canoe and rowed towards them. Neon recognised her red hair instantly – only it was a little messier than normal, sticking almost bolt upright like she had been electrocuted.

'Filly!' Neon cried. 'Filly, thank the unicorns you're

here! Quick, Filly, SAVE ME!'

Much to Neon's surprise, Filly muttered, 'Oh no,' and began rowing back the way she had just come!

'Wait! I know her ...' Neon said, pushing past the kelpies to get to Filly. As she swam closer she could see Filly's face was covered in fish and she had some globs of goo stuck up her nose.

'Neon,' Filly growled. 'What are you doing here?'

'Filly!' Neon cried. 'You've got ... fish on your face. Loads of them.'

'Yes, Neon,' Filly said with a snap. 'That's because I did not have the right comb. You sold me the wrong comb and now I have to spend the entire holiday with little fish on my face. And let me tell you, not only do they stink but they talk about the MOST ANNOYING THINGS ... yes, you do. Don't argue with me just because you're stuck on my face! No, I will not be quiet, it's MY FACE!'

'You've also got goo up your nose,' Neon said quietly.

'I DID THAT MYSELF TO HELP WITH THE FISH SMELL.'

'Right,' Neon said. 'Um …' she looked back and saw the army of kelpies snaking towards her. 'Could I jump in? It's a long story but I don't have a comb and I don't want them to attack me.'

'NO!' Filly cried, rowing out of grasp. 'First you sell me a dangerously wrong comb, then you embarrass me at a really exclusive Twizzle goo brewing class and now you're pestering me ON MY GOO CANOE.'

'Yes,' Neon said quickly, trying to inch closer to the canoe. Under the surface she could feel more kelpies brushing against her legs. 'I need to get to Lumino – but my PORTAL OPENER IS BROKEN! I don't have time to explain but let's just say I know a big and dangerous secret and I think there's someone here who might be about to destroy everything.'

'I believe you,' Filly said.

'Oh good,' Neon said, reaching out a hand so Filly could pull her in.

'You're probably the one who will destroy everything! You've certainly ruined my holiday!'

The kelpies weaved closer.

'Please,' Neon begged, splash-swimming along by the side of the goo canoe, swallowing clumps of goo and spluttering as she went.

'No,' Filly said.

'Please,' Neon said, swimming closer.

'No.'

'Please?'

'NO!'

A glob of goo hit Neon's face and the kelpies cackled.

'What was … ?' Neon said slowly, wiping off the goo. 'OH MY UNICORNS, WHAT IS THAT SMELL?!'

When they arrived at Sprinkle Lodge Campgrounds, Geldie met them with a raised eyebrow.

The place was peppered with glittery trees, their huge canopies hanging low over gooey tents and crackling campfires. It smelt of fish BECAUSE THAT WAS ALL NEON COULD SMELL. Through the trees she could just make out the soupy purple lagoon. Under the surface, the kelpies' eyes lit up like monstrous fireflies.

'Neon … you're in Lumino Falls?' Geldie said. 'And you're … covered in tiny fish. And so are you, Filly. It isn't because—'

'Wrong comb,' and 'No comb,' Filly and Neon said at the same time.

'Oh,' Geldie said, producing a comb and holding it aloft. 'Neon did actually ask me to bring you the correct comb, Filly. But I couldn't find you.'

'TOO LATE,' Filly snapped as a fish slapped its tail on to her eye.

'And why are you here, Neon?' Geldie dared to ask.

'My portal opener got damp and brought me here, but that's not important,' Neon rambled. 'I know a secret, Geldie! A terrible secret about a Long-Lost Unicorn Hunter, and they are here – here in the UNIverse, and I think they might be about to let the UHs in and destroy everything!'

'Are you talking about the legend of the Long-Lost Unicorn Hunter?' came a voice behind them.

Neon spun round to find Greg, Geldie's dad and the

82

most famous unicorn in the world – the one who made up the horses with horns – standing behind them!

'You know that secret?' Neon said.

'Oh yeah,' Greg said. 'It's the scariest secret in the UNIverse. Hardly anyone knows it. The Gooheads mentioned it once, by accident, and I've never forgotten it.'

'THERE'S A UNICORN HUNTER *IN THE UNIverse*?' Geldie cried, ducking as if one might be hovering above him at that very second.

'Let's light the campfire,' Greg said. 'And I'll tell you the whole story – the whole terribly terrifying story.'

10

Scary Story Round the Goofire

G reg and Geldie had a goo camper. A gooey-looking campervan-type vehicle, kitted out with a Volefizz fridge and little gooey curtains. Outside was a crackling campfire and some squidgy seats.

'Take a seat, Neon,' Greg said kindly.

'Throw some more goo on the fire, Geldie,' Greg added. 'Oh wait, throw this one, it'll help with my story.'

Neon glanced at the label.

SPOOKY GOOFIRE STORY ENHANCER GOO

Neon pulled a blanket around her shoulders and settled down to hear the story. The whole horrible lot of it.

'The legend of the Long-Lost Unicorn Hunter is a tale no one has heard,' Greg said excitedly, as the fire began to spark.

'Apart from Neon, who heard it from a talking sweet or something,' Filly pointed out.

'Yes,' Greg said. 'Apart from Neon. I heard it as a boy, not long after I invented the horse-with-a-horn idea. I don't think I was meant to hear them talking about it, but this is what they said ...'

In the fire, Neon could see a tiny figure cloaked in flames.

'Um,' she said, pointing. 'There's a tiny figure in there.'

'That's the Story Enhancer goo at work,' Greg explained. 'The fire will show the story.'

'Oh,' Neon said, leaning in closer.

'Half a century ago there lived a child,' Greg said eerily, while the little figure in the fire opted for a less atmospheric approach and waved at them all enthusiastically instead.

'I got the Story Enhancer goo from the discount section in the Goomart,' Greg said apologetically. 'So it might not work properly.'

The little figure in the fire nodded in agreement

and then got back to waving.

'Anyway, where was I?' Greg said, throwing the little figure in the fire an annoyed look. 'Ah yes. This child lived along the road from two of the deadliest Unicorn Hunters in the world! And they had been told a prophecy that all UHs have been told ever since.'

The little figure in the fire began opening and closing his mouth to indicate the telling of a prophecy, but Neon thought he looked like he was mimicking a fish.

'The prophecy said,' Greg went on, 'that this child would join their ranks, secretly, and then find a path to the UNIverse. You see, the child had no family, but a kindly unicorn would take him in and show him the ways of their world, never knowing the child was an UH.'

They all gasped!

'And there they would wait, growing older as the years passed,' Greg said as the little figure in the fire stood on his tiptoes, 'before one day, rising up. They would open a portal for the UHs to enter. Thereby DESTROYING THE UNIverse FROM THE INSIDE OUT!'

The fire exploded and the little figure walked out

from the flames, whispering, 'I am the Long-Lost Unicorn Hunter.'

The little figure's face was clear to Neon now. It was Greg!

'Is that you?' Neon asked.

'Yeah, because I'm telling the story. The mini version of me is acting out the story,' Greg said as the little figure disappeared with a *pop*.

'That's a terrifying story,' Geldie said with a shiver.

'It's probably not true though, is it?' Filly said.

Neon leaned in closer to the fire, her face alight with fear. 'It's real. And now the time has come for the Long-Lost Unicorn Hunter to rise up and destroy the UNIverse, just like the prophecy said – from the inside out.'

11

Kelpgoos Department Store

Filly's reaction to Neon's dramatic statement was to take her shopping.

'I don't have time for shopping!' Neon cried. 'Didn't you hear? The whole UNIverse is in danger, and I need to get back to Lumino and warn people! We need to find out who the Long-Lost Unicorn Hunter is. Old Lady Buck might know, she's been around for ages ...'

'It's not actually shopping,' Filly scoffed. 'If we're going to get you to Lumino quickly, the easiest way is to borrow the goo canoe sea monster and fly back there on him. He's like a torpedo. But he's owned by the kelpies, so you'll have to get their permission. It's holiday season, so they won't give him up easily – he gets them so many combs at this time of year. We just need one of them to put in a good word for us with the kelpie boss.'

'And how exactly does SHOPPING help us do this?'
Neon asked with exasperation.

'Well, because there are lots of kelpies here to ask, and anyway I need to go shopping for something to hide my fish face.'

'Filly!' Neon cried.

'What?' Filly said. 'It's your fault, *remember*?'

Neon stared down into the gloopy purple lagoon. Deep down below she could see a flashing sign, spiky and unfriendly, and it read:

KELPGOOS DEPARTMENT STORE:
IT'S NOT FOR YOU!

Diving into goo was something Neon was quite used to, she'd done plenty of it back in Lumino – from diving into the SWIMMING POOL OF DOOM goo at the Goomart to the fish tanks at Whiskers & Gloop. But she was completely unprepared for shopping at Kelpgoos.

'NO, YOU'RE NOT ALLOWED TO BUY THOSE!

YOU CAN'T BUY ANYTHING!' the kelpie said, grabbing the jelly shoes Neon had picked up.

'I was just looking,' Neon said.

'NO LOOKING! GO AWAY!'

'This is a really odd department store,' Neon said, as she watched a customer's hair being pulled as she attempted to purchase a pool float.

'Yeah,' Filly said, completely unfazed. 'Kelpies are really unfriendly.'

The whole place floated like a submarine in the purple lagoon and each department was peppered with *GO AWAY* signs and various other insults. Blobs of purple goo dripped from the seams in the ceiling and Neon got the unnerving feeling the lagoon was readying to burst at any second.

The place was alive with clattering and shouts and the sound of things smashing. In the toy department, things were going flying. Over in the holiday section, pool floats were being burst by furious kelpies shouting, 'NO! NOT FOR YOU!' And next to Neon in the shoe section, a kelpie was *eating* shoes.

'NOM NOM NOM, CAN'T BUY THE SHOES BECAUSE THEY ARE IN MY BELLY NOW! HAHAHAHA!'

'Can we go?' Neon asked. 'There must be another way. In fact, I'm going to guess we'll *need* to find another way, because they are never going to do us a favour.'

'Everyone has a price,' Filly said. 'Even kelpies from an escaped Scottish Legends goo.'

'Filly,' Neon said sternly. 'They have covered our faces in fish that will not come off and absolutely stink. And one just *ate* some shoes. They are *not* going to do us a favour.'

'GET OUT GET OUT GET OUT GET OUT GET OUT GET OUT,' one chanted in Neon's ear.

Neon backed up. It was hard to move through goo. She hit a display case. A jar of goo slipped to the rocky ground and smashed. A tiny glob of goo seeped out.

'Uh-oh,' Neon whispered. She picked up what remained of the jar.

ANGRY HAIRY MONSTER GOO

92

'Just what I need,' Neon said, rolling her eyes. She'd met this goo before.

'FEED ME BRAINS!' came a squeak as a tiny hairy monster emerged from the goo. 'FEED ME BRAINS!' it cried again, lunging at Neon and biting her earlobe.

'This is a disaster,' she groaned. But much to her surprise, the kelpies started laughing and clapping.

'What's happening?' Neon whispered.

'They love a laugh,' Filly said, as if that was a good explanation.

'OW!' The monster bit Neon's nose.

The kelpies began hugging her and patting her on the back.

'I don't really understand it,' Filly said with a shrug, 'but laughter is the best medicine … if you're being attacked by kelpies. Or so the saying goes.'

The kelpies wiped the fish from both their faces.

'I knew you'd make them laugh,' Filly said.

'Why didn't you try to make them laugh if you knew that's all we had to do to get rid of the fish?' Neon cried.

'Trust me, I tried,' Filly explained. 'But I am humourless.'

'No you're not,' Neon said. 'You're funny in your own way. You know jokes!'

Filly turned, stern-faced, and looked at a kelpie who was eagerly awaiting the joke.

'What is green and yellow and scaly all over?'

'I don't know!' the kelpie squealed with glee. 'Tell me! Tell me!'

'A fish, specifically a fish species from the blue goo lagoon, first discovered in the early Uni-period. The fish even have scaly eyelids – fascinating and rather hilarious, yes? Especially when you hear their name – Scaly Fish Eyes Fish. '

'NO! NOT HILARIOUS!' The kelpie stuck out her tongue and snaked off.

'See what I mean?' Filly said.

'FEED ME BRAINS!' the little hairy monster squealed, kicking Neon's lips.

'*Why*,' Neon breathed, 'didn't you *tell me* this when they FIRST PUT FISH ON MY FACE?!'

'Because I wanted you to see what it's like – call it REVENGE,' Filly said.

'AAAAARGH,' Neon roared. 'Filly, the whole UNIverse is in danger! I need to get back to Lumino, the Gooheads need to know. I have things to do!'

The kelpies all roared with laughter.

'It's not funny,' Neon said, which made them laugh even more.

'I think it's because the tiny hairy monster is bouncing on your head,' Filly said, cracking a rare smile. 'And anyway, I was telling the truth about the goo canoe monster. This is your quickest route home.'

Neon threw her hands in the air. 'Fine, it's all hilarious. Now, can one of you go to the kelpie boss and please ask if I can borrow the sea monster who rents out the goo canoes? I need him for a quick flight.'

12

Spectacular Views

Aboard an airfancy – what unicorns call their gooey aeroplanes – the passengers were enjoying a cool Volefizz and spectacular views of Lumino lit up in an emerald haze. But that peaceful scene was soon interrupted by a young girl in tie-dye tights screaming at the top of her lungs as she shot past at lightning speed on top of a round and incredibly slimy flying monster holding an assortment of canoes.

Old Lady Buck thanked the goo canoe monster and the kelpies on Neon's behalf by gifting him every comb in the Goomart.

Moya held Neon upright while she tried to regain her balance – her eyes were rolling about in her

head from the ride.

'Why the rush?' Old Lady Buck asked, and Neon didn't waste a second. She told her everything and watched as the old woman's eyes grew wider and wider and her jaw inched closer and closer to the floor.

'We must find out who the Long-Lost Unicorn Hunter is,' Old Lady Buck said. 'And fast.'

'Oh,' Neon said, her shoulders sagging sadly. 'I

thought you might already know who it was, since you're so ol— ... WISE.'

Old Lady Buck raised an amused eyebrow. 'I have no clue, and for once I am at a loss as to where to begin.'

'Well,' Neon said, 'this Mr Ragwort character obviously knows who the Long-Lost Unicorn Hunter is, so maybe I should start with him.'

'Do we have any clues as to who it could be?' Old Lady Buck asked. 'Did the Mystica sweet say anything else?'

Neon wracked her brains – she'd been so focused on the fact that a Unicorn Hunter existed in the UNIverse she had completely forgotten the other stuff.

'Yes!' Neon cried, recalling what she had read. '*THEY CAN BE FOUND BENEATH THE GOO. BUT THEY DON'T HIDE IN THE SHADOWS, THEY ARE KNOWN, THEY ARE SEEN.*'

'Found beneath the goo?' Bronco said, racing past, closely followed by a roller-skating vampire. 'That could be anywhere!' he said, doubling back. 'The UNIverse is full of goo – could be the gooey sky, the gooey waters, under a gooey roof, or a gooey tent.'

Old Lady Buck shook her head. 'He's right. That doesn't mean much. *They are known, they are seen* is more interesting to me. Could it be someone famous?'

Neon gasped. 'Twizzle!' she cried.

'The celebrity chef attached to the fabulous moustache?' Moya said. 'What makes you think it's him?'

'Well, you reach the Strange Goo Society by diving beneath some goo,' Neon said. 'NOT THAT HE'S A MEMBER – I DIDN'T TELL YOU THAT. And he's known and he's seen – he's a celebrity chef!'

Old Lady Buck narrowed her eyes. 'You *could* be right.'

'I must be!' Neon said. 'It makes perfect sense.'

'So he's going to let the Unicorn Hunters in?' Moya asked. 'When?'

'According to Mr Ragwort,' Neon said gravely, 'it's going to happen soon.'

'All right, unicorns,' Old Lady Buck said. Menace Goo Smasher nuzzled into her. 'No, not you, Menace Goo Smasher, us *real* ones. We've got to act fast. Neon, go back to the human world and see what you can find out about the plan from Mr Ragwort. Take this goo – it'll help. And leave Twizzle to me.'

'But my portal opener …' Neon said. 'It got wet and it's not working.'

'I can help!' Moya cried. She began frantically eating a chocolate snowball. 'MON MIT!' she said, accidentally spitting some chocolate at Neon.

A small splodge of chocolate landed on Neon's wrist, but no one noticed.

The portal fizzed and crackled and burst open in front of them.

'No,' Old Lady Buck said, pushing Moya through the portal to the human world and then pulling her back again so the portal closed. 'We need you here. Take Menace Goo Smasher to Lumino Falls and get Filly, Geldie and Greg to come back – we're going to need all the help we can get.'

She turned to Neon and took her lipstick. Carefully she dried it on her apron. 'Haven't you heard of water damage, my dear – nothing a little drying out can't fix.'

She held the lipstick in the air and inspected it. 'That should do it.'

Neon drew a portal with her lipstick and it fizzed open. She popped her head through – it was her bedroom!

'All right,' Neon said. 'Let's do this.'

'Unicorns,' Old Lady Buck said. 'This is for the UNIverse.'

'FOR THE UNIverse!' Moya cried. 'GO UNICORNS! GO UNICORNS! GO UNICORNS! GO UNICORNS! GO UNICORNS! GO, GO, GO!'

'Too much, Moya,' Old Lady Buck said, patting her on the back.

THE GLOOPY

*Lumino's No. 1 mag, where goo
and style collide!*

HOW TO BE MORE HUMICORN!

Our favourite and only humicorn, Neon Gallup, was seen soaring through the skies in spectacular style. Get the look with the following:

1. Cool tie-dye tights and a black dress.
2. Add a screaming face of unrelenting fear.
3. Make sure to accessorise with a goo monster.
4. Add canoes.

13

A New Unicorn Hunter

Neon sat behind the counter in Ratty's clutching her lipstick tightly in her pocket. Across the room, in their usual corner, sat the UHs. She looked from them to the clock – the day was going so slowly! All she wanted was to be back in the UNIverse. Had they found Twizzle? Had they stopped the Long-Lost Unicorn Hunter?

Neon's eyes widened. 'I have an idea!'

'Pardon?' one of the UHs called over.

'I … um …' She hadn't meant to say it out loud. But it didn't hugely matter because her idea involved *them*.

She walked over confidently. 'I want to be an UH.'

'We don't really need any extra help at this stage – this is the end game, we're about to fulfil our life's mission and destroy the unicorns once and for all.'

'I can help by … giving you free ratpuccinos?' Neon squeaked.

'She's in, she's an UH,' Mr Ragwort said.

'WHAT?' Priscilla cried. 'No, she can't join, she's a …'

Neon waited for Priscilla to finish her sentence, but, strangely, she didn't.

'I don't see why Neon can't join,' Mrs Knackerman said. 'Especially if it means we get free ratpuccinos.'

Neon made a mental note to apologise to her parents for that one at a later date. She made a fresh brew over at the coffee machine and, checking no one was watching her, tipped in the goo Old Lady Buck had given her. She glanced at the label.

TRUTH GOO

'Priscilla, give Neon a T-shirt,' Mrs Knackerman ordered as Neon made her way over to the table with the goo-filled coffee cup. 'It's UH club policy that we now wear them at all times,' Mrs Knackerman said to Neon.

'Uh-huh, all times,' Neon mumbled as she placed the cup down carefully in front of Mr Ragwort.

Priscilla held out the T-shirt to Neon, but when Neon grabbed it, Priscilla didn't let go.

They wrestled with it in silence, each pulling so tightly it looked like it might rip.

'PRISCILLA!' Mrs Knackerman snapped. She wrenched the T-shirt from her grasp and gave it to Neon. 'I'm sorry, Neon, I don't know what's got into her lately. I found her sleeping in the middle of her bedroom this morning – she'd moved the bed. And do you know what? She said she didn't!'

Neon knew that, of course. She didn't know why Priscilla wasn't telling them Neon was a unicorn though. Maybe she thought they wouldn't believe her?

'Oops, Neon,' Mrs Knackerman said. 'You've got some melted chocolate on your wrist.'

'Oh, that must be from Moya's chocolate snowballs,' Neon said, her mind on Mr Ragwort and the cup of truth goo. She took a napkin and wiped the chocolate off, then she took a seat between Priscilla and Mr

Ragwort and beamed. Her plan was working! If there was a Unicorn Hunter hiding in the UNIverse, why couldn't she be a unicorn hiding among the Unicorn Hunters?

Mr Ragwort took a sip of the ratpuccino and the results of the goo were instantaneous.

'Mr Ragwort, would you like to begin the meeting?' Mrs Knackerman said.

'NO I WOULD NOT,' Mr Ragwort declared loudly. 'DESPITE MY BRAVADO, I FIND PUBLIC SPEAK-ING INTIMIDATING.'

'Um, all right,' Mrs Knackerman said.

Neon didn't waste any time. 'What is the plan with the Unicorn Hunter in the UNIverse? When are they going to strike? What are they going to do?'

Mr Ragwort turned slowly to Neon. For a second she worried the goo had worn off. Maybe you only got one truth and all she'd find out was that he didn't like public speaking!

But the truth goo was stronger than that, and she was in luck. Sort of.

'I HAVE ABSOLUTELY NO IDEA,' he boomed.

'What?' Neon said quietly.

'I KNOW AS MUCH AS EVERYONE ELSE – WHICH IS NOTHING! I JUST LIKE TO PRETEND I KNOW MORE TO FEEL IMPORTANT.'

'So there's no plan with the Long-Lost Unicorn Hunter? You don't know them?' Neon pressed.

'NO! ALL I KNOW IS THE SAME AS EVERYONE ELSE – THE STORY OF THE LONG-LOST UNICORN HUNTER. Everyone's been waiting for him to rise up and let us in. But I don't know him personally.'

'I do,' Mrs Knackerman said. 'I've lived in this town all my life and he lived next door – in Neon's house. He was called—'

'Twizzle!' Neon gasped.

'What a weird name. Why on earth would you think that?' Mrs Knackerman looked confused. 'No, he was called Greg.'

Neon choked. 'GREG?'

Mrs Knackerman shrugged. 'Is that so surprising? It's a normal name.'

Neon got up from the table so quickly she knocked the whole thing over.

'NEON!' Mrs Knackerman cried.

Cups smashed, cuddly toy rats rolled across the floor. The goo ratpuccino flew into the air and rained down on them. Neon watched in horror as a single droplet of the coffee landed in Priscilla's gaping mouth!

'NOOOOOOO!' Neon cried – Priscilla was the very last person in the world she wanted anywhere near a TRUTH GOO. But it was too late.

Priscilla rose to her feet silently and pointed at Neon.

'NEON GALLUP IS—'

'WONDERFUL! NEON IS GREAT! THANKS, PRISCILLA, WOW, YOU'RE SO KIND,' Neon rambled in a desperate attempt to distract her.

'SHE'S A—' Priscilla stopped.

Neon breathed a sigh of relief. But it was for nothing. Priscilla had stopped because there was a fizzing sound coming from the floor behind them. Glitter was erupting from … a napkin.

'THE CHOCOLATE!' Neon cried. She'd wiped the

chocolate off her wrist – but the chocolate was from Moya's portal opener. It wouldn't open a portal on a person, but since she'd wiped it off …

'Oh no!' she cried, smacking a hand to her forehead.

The portal was already huge and it was getting bigger, and fast.

The UHs sat in stunned silence.

'It's happening,' Mr Ragwort said in disbelief. 'The Long-Lost Unicorn Hunter has opened a portal for us!'

Neon stood in front of it, trying to hide it, to distract them, anything! Sprays of glitter shot through her hair. Stars *pinged* off her back.

'Well, Neon,' Mrs Knackerman said, shoving her out of the way, her eyes wide and wild. 'You picked an exciting day to join the UHs!'

Then something really strange happened to the UHs. As they got to their feet, their eyes began to flash red.

All Neon could do was watch on helplessly as one by one they lined up and stepped through the portal!

She stood next to the swirling vortex in the deathly silence of the empty cafe, unable to move or speak or even scream. Not only had she just let the UHs into the UNIverse but the portal was growing bigger. *Moya's* snowball had opened it and she needed Moya to close it or it was going to get bigger and bigger until everyone in the world knew about the UNIverse!

By a stroke of unusual luck, only seconds later, Moya stuck her head through the portal.

'Neon,' she said, jumping through. 'Old Lady Buck got Twizzle! She captured him. He's in the back room of the Goomart as we speak. Come on!'

Much to Neon's relief, the portal closed. She whipped out her lipstick and opened another portal.

'Why is your hand trembling?' Moya asked, but Neon didn't answer. How was she going to tell them all? How was she going to break it to them that it was all over? The UHs were in the UNIverse. The very worst thing that could ever happen HAD HAPPENED.

14

Greg Didn't Get the Memo

When Moya and Neon arrived in the Goomart, Twizzle was gooed to a chair with Old Lady Buck and Greg looming over him.

'Oh no,' Neon said. 'Um, guys, he's not—'

'YOU *ARE* THE LONG-LOST UNICORN HUNTER,' Old Lady Buck roared.

'No, I'm not!' Twizzle protested. 'I don't even know what that means. But I'm *not*.'

Old Lady Buck inspected a goo jar. 'This truth goo must be out of date.'

'It's not,' Neon said. 'He's not—'

'We could try this one?' Greg said, handing Old Lady Buck another jar.

'Dad,' Geldie said, trying to grab the jar back. 'INTIMIDATING SPIDER goo feels entirely unnecessary. Not to mention the fact they're hard to clean up and Bronco is—'

'DON'T MAKE ME CLEAN UP AN INTIMIDATING SPIDER GOO,' Bronco pleaded.

'PLEASE!' Twizzle squealed. 'I'm not the Long-Lost Unicorn Hunter! I'm a humble chef! A humble, talented, award-winning chef!'

'You *are* the Long-Lost Unicorn Hunter,' Old Lady Buck said, twisting off the jar lid. 'You will betray us all and we're going to stop you!'

'NO, PLEASE!' Twizzle and Bronco both cried at once.

'STOP!' Neon shouted, standing between Old Lady Buck and Twizzle. 'WILL YOU ALL JUST LISTEN TO ME FOR A SECOND?'

The others stared at her in surprise.

'He's right. He's not the Long-Lost Unicorn Hunter,' Neon said.

'But you were the one who made the suggestion in the first place,' Old Lady Buck said.

Neon held her hands in the air. 'I was wrong, but

113

I know who it is now.'

'Who?' Greg asked.

'It's *you*.' She turned to face him.

Greg looked at her in shock.

'He lives below the goo – you have a gooey roof, don't you?'

'Same as everyone else in Little Trot,' Old Lady Buck said, jumping to his defence.

'And you are known, you are *seen*,' Neon went on. 'Since inventing the horse-with-a-horn, everyone knows you – your face is on the gold coins, your face is on buildings. You're the most seen unicorn in the UNIverse.'

Everyone fell silent, apart from Filly, who grabbed some popcorn goo and said, 'Ooh, plot twist.'

Geldie stood up, the colour draining from his face. 'Dad,' he whispered. 'You said you were an orphan. You don't remember your early childhood. Are you an UH?!'

Greg looked off into the distance, his face scrunched in confusion. 'I don't have many memories of my time in the human world, but I do vaguely remember a group

114

of people in matching T-shirts saying I could join their club …'

'DAD!' Geldie roared. 'YOU'RE EVIL!'

'No I'm not,' he said. 'You've discovered my secret though. I'm not a unicorn. It's why I've never quite fitted in – I'm terrible at goo. But I saved the UNIverse – I invented the horse-with-a-horn. And mullet hairdos to hide the stripe of hair.'

'Wait,' Neon said. 'So you don't have a plan to let the UHs in?'

'NO!' Greg cried. 'I'd never betray my friends and destroy my home – never! I didn't even like the T-shirt they gave me!'

'I think that's what you were meant to do, you know, let them in,' Filly said. 'You're meant to be evil.'

'Well, I didn't get the memo,' Greg said defiantly.

Old Lady Buck chuckled. 'Greg is the Long-Lost UH. And he also happens to be the hero of the UNIverse. I think we're safe.' She breathed a big sigh of relief.

'We're safe!' Moya cheered.

'Um, about that …' Neon blushed.

'SO THIS IS THEIR MENACING SHOP OF GOO MAGIC!' came a cry.

They all turned to see Mr Ragwort and the other UHs inspecting the Goomart shelves.

'I, um,' Neon said quietly, 'have some really bad news ...'

15

UH-oh

Inside the Goomart, the UHs marched about, their mouths agog at the place.

'They seem impressed, at least,' Old Lady Buck said.

Neon watched Priscilla pick up a discount cheese goo and sniff it.

'What are we going to do?' Neon whispered. 'We can't just hide in the back room forever.'

They all looked at Greg.

'I'm really only good at fun, creative solutions to problems,' he whispered. 'This looks like it's going to require combat.'

Neon held her breath as an UH stalked past, not noticing the slightly ajar door or all the eyes peering out.

'Combat?' she whispered. 'Surely they aren't that

bad? They're just normal human townsfolk with an obsession.'

Geldie grabbed Neon's arm, his eyes wide with fear. 'Neon, you don't know UHs.'

Priscilla smashed the jar, and a walking talking cheese in platform shoes burst from the puddle of goo.

Neon smiled smugly. That would be enough to send them running home, surely.

'Should I open a portal back to the human world?' she said confidently. 'I'm positive they'll want to leave soon after seeing a giant annoying cheese!'

But the others continued to look terrified.

'It's bad, I know,' she continued. 'And now the secret's out it's going to be hard to contain in the human world. But there are solutions, I'm sure! Let's not get too scared. Discovering our secret was the very worst that could happen. I'm actually feeling quite relieved – the worst has happened but everything will be O—'

She was interrupted by an ear-piercing scream, followed by the sound of stampeding platforms.

Neon peeked out and watched in horror as the cheese ran in the opposite direction. Priscilla's eyes flashed red and she raised her hands in the air. With one swish of her thumb, the cheese melted into a puddle of goo.

'Wait,' Neon said. 'Priscilla, she has … she has POWERS?'

The others nodded.

'You mean, in the UNIverse, UHs are powerful?' Neon wheezed. She could barely breathe.

'Very,' Geldie said gravely.

'But they're only humans,' Neon said.

Filly prodded her. 'Pay attention, Neon, they're UHs. They might just be humans in the human world, but in the UNIverse UHs are superhuman. Why do you think unicorns are so worried about them?'

Neon watched as Mrs Knackerman shot red goo from her eyes. It splattered across the walls, making them crack and turn to goo.

'Wait,' Neon said. 'I *technically* joined the UHs. I was trying to get information from them, but then

I opened the portal. Does this mean I'll develop monster powers?'

Filly laughed.

'No, dear,' Old Lady Buck said. 'You might've become a member of the UH club, but true UHs are *born* as UHs. Either you are one or you're not. It's the same reason Greg didn't develop powers when he entered the UNIverse, despite joining the club and getting the T-shirt.'

'Oh,' Neon said, watching the Goomart crumble as the UHs tested out their powers.

'You know, the funny thing is,' Old Lady Buck said, 'even the UHs didn't know they'd get such strange powers when they came here ... but they do now.'

They shot more red goo from their eyes and mouths and ears and they made things move by twisting their fingers. Priscilla's head did a full 360 degree turn!

Neon screamed. Roller-skating vampires tore past, skating – for the first time ever – in fear. A FEED ME BRAINS! monster came running towards them and hid in Greg's hair.

Among the UHs were one or two normal humans who had obviously joined the UHs for fun. They were cowering at the sight of the UHs' transformation, their faces painted with fear and red goo. The whole place was chaos. Unicorn customers bolted through the door, still carrying their little shopping baskets, spilling the panic out on to the street. Outside, shrieks sounded and the town bell tolled a warning.

Neon couldn't believe it. In the UNIverse, the UHs weren't odd, unicorn-hunting, portal-digging outcasts. In the UNIverse they were powerful. In the UNIverse they were MONSTERS.

'We've gotta get out of here,' Neon cried and they raced for the door.

But Old Lady Buck stayed put. She looked at them and smiled.

'I'm not leaving my Goomart, Neon.'

'But Old Lady Buck, you won't survive.'

The old unicorn held her head high.

The sound of Santa shouting 'HO HO HO RUN FOR YOUR LIVES!' echoed through the Goomart.

'Oh no, they've got to the festive section,' Neon said. Terrified snowmen bounced past, followed by a herd of screaming elves.

Neon felt the tears welling in her eyes. She wiped them away furiously. 'You have to come with us,' she pleaded with Old Lady Buck as the ceiling began to crumble.

'Go and save the UNIverse!' Old Lady Buck said as the UHs turned to Neon. Their eyes glowed red and fierce, and slippery red goo shot from them, coating everything in sight!

'RUN!' Old Lady Buck shouted, smacking Menace Goo Smasher on the bottom. The gooey unicorn charged at them, knocking Neon outside.

She hit the pavement with a *bang* just as the Goomart's glorious doors swung shut.

All across town, panic was setting in.

'Take a goo pet, save yourselves!' the owner of Whiskers & Gloop cried, throwing pet cubes and eggs on to the street. One landed in Neon's lap – a little egg filled with lime-green goo, with tiny wings carved on

the shell. But Neon was too distracted to notice. She stared at the Goomart and watched in horror as one by one the walls turned to goo. Beyond the window, she could see Old Lady Buck standing strong in the middle of the store, chucking goo at the UHs, fighting them off. But it was no good. The last thing Neon saw before the others dragged her away was Old Lady Buck disappearing beneath a tidal wave of red goo.

16

The Wobbly Under

Neon was silent as they charged through the streets of Lumino. Panic was spreading far and wide as all around them shutters came down and doors were bolted shut.

'I know a place we can go!' Greg shouted. 'It once belonged to the Gooheads, but it's completely abandoned now. They won't mind us popping in and hiding for our lives.'

Neon was lost in her own thoughts. 'I had no idea they'd be so ...'

'Terrifying? Destructive? Unicorn Huntery?' Moya shouted down from atop Menace Goo Smasher.

'Competent,' Neon panted. She had a question she wanted to ask and it was weighing so heavily on her that she couldn't hold it in any longer. 'Do you think

Old Lady Buck is … OK?'

Moya bit her lip to stop herself from crying.

'Oh, she's a goner, Neon,' Filly said, running up beside her. 'And it's all your fault.'

'It is!' Neon wailed.

'Filly!' Geldie said as he tried to keep up. 'That's not nice.'

'No,' Filly said. 'What's not nice is living in a town full of Unicorn Hunters and portal-jumping back and forth to the UNIverse like everything's fine and THEN letting a bunch of Unicorn Hunters in to destroy everything. THAT,' she said, pointing at Neon, 'is not nice.'

Neon hung her head in shame. Then suddenly, she felt something sharp in her hand. She unfurled her fingers to see the little mystery pet egg she was clutching had begun to glow and crack. She watched in astonishment as goo seeped out and fused with her hand.

'We're here!' Greg said, as Moya pulled Menace Goo Smasher to an abrupt halt.

Neon looked up at the building. 'No,' she whimpered.

GOOHEAD CENTRAL.

'I can't go in there,' Neon protested. She knew that the Gooheads, the rulers of the UNIverse, would have no sympathy with her for accidentally letting UHs in. They'd send her to the goo pits for life, or worse!

'We're not going in there,' Greg said. 'We're going to the Wobbly Under.'

And he marched off towards the building as if that should mean something to them.

'Huh?' Moya said.

'The Wobbly whatta?' Geldie mumbled.

'I have serious concerns about putting our lives in *Greg's* hands,' Filly said.

Wobble went Menace Goo Smasher.

'What's the Wobbly Under?' Neon asked.

Filly turned to her and glared. 'Do these look like the faces of unicorns who know?'

'Come on!' Greg said, calling them over to a carving of his own face on the wall.

'Does it ever weird you out that your dad saved the

UNIverse and so his face will be everywhere forever?'
Moya asked Geldie.

'Maybe the UHs will add Neon's face to everything
when they take over. You know, because she
DESTROYED IT,' Filly said, storming off towards
Greg.

'She's never going to forgive me, is she?' Neon said
sadly.

'Ah, we might all be dead soon,' Moya said. 'So it
won't matter.'

They dashed over to see what Greg was doing.
Strangely, he was knocking on the carving of his face –
focusing on the nose.

'It's definitely around here somewhere,' he mumbled.

Neon looked to Geldie for answers but Geldie only
shrugged.

'Dad …' Geldie said slowly. 'You got a shock seeing
the UHs, maybe you're not feeling very well and hitting
the wall is—'

'Aha!' Greg cried, and much to everyone's surprise
goo began to drip down the wall, cascading from the

nose and collecting in the carving's bottom lip like a little fountain. Then came a *pop* and the nose extended and twisted into the shape of a handle. Greg heaved it open to reveal a dark abyss beyond.

'Where does it lead?' Neon asked nervously.

'The Wobbly Under!' Greg cheered. 'Just like I told you.'

'But none of us knows what you mean,' Geldie said faintly.

'Step inside, little unicorns,' Greg said. 'This is a passageway to the most secret place in Lumino ...'

Beyond the secret entrance lay a slimy room, and in that slimy room Neon was horrified to find ...

The Gooheads!

(If you've not met them before, they really are four heads. In goo.)

Neon SCREAMED!

The Gooheads screamed back.

'AAAARGH!'

'Why are we screaming?' the green Goohead screamed.

'Because Neon is screaming,' the yellow head screamed. 'It's only polite.'

Neon turned to run, but the door had vanished.

'What are you doing here, Gooheads?' Greg said in astonishment, his arms wide as if he were greeting old friends.

'What do you think we're doing here?' the purple head said flatly.

'Holiday?' Greg guessed.

The Gooheads rolled their eyes in unison.

'We're here because of the UHs, *obviously*.'

'Ah!' Greg said. 'Us too.'

'They are growing more powerful,' the purple head said gravely. 'With every minute an UH spends in the UNIverse they grow more monstrous.'

Neon gulped. The Gooheads turned to face her and fixed her with a stern stare.

'Any idea how a herd of UHs from Brunty wandered so effortlessly through a portal to the UNIverse, Neon?'

Neon gulped again. 'I do ... not know,' she lied.

The Gooheads, much to her surprise, turned away from her.

'That was easy,' she whispered to Moya. But then she realised that's who the Gooheads were focused on.

'Moya McGlow,' the blue head said. 'Our goostincts tell us it was *you* who opened the portal.'

'Oh no, it wasn't—' Neon tried to interject.

'NEON GALLUP, BE QUIET!' the purple head bellowed.

'Um,' Moya said. 'I don't think I did? I'm quite forgetful though, so can I choose MAYBE as an option, or is this a straightforward YES or NO question?'

'We're disappointed,' the yellow head said. 'You have single-handedly caused the greatest crisis in UNIverse history.'

'WAIT A MINUTE!' Filly roared. 'Moya wasn't—'

'FILLY SPANGLE, BE QUIET!!' the blue head bellowed so loudly Filly fell over and bounced across the floor.

Neon stepped forward. 'It was my cafe – Ratty's, you know, the one with the rat theme? I live in Brunty. I was there when the portal opened. I was the reason it opened.'

'But it was Moya's chocolate snowball that opened the portal,' the yellow head said. 'We Gooheads *know* that to be true.'

'Yes, it was, *technically*,' Neon said. 'But it was my fault.'

The Gooheads turned back to Neon.

'Both of you will be punished then.'

'No, just me,' Neon insisted.

Filly gave an exasperated groan, and then much to everyone's surprise, she lifted the purple Goohead and stuffed it in a cupboard.

'What are you doing, Filly Spangle?!' the blue head yelled as Filly marched back and shoved him in the cupboard too. She kept going until all four of them were lined up neatly inside, and then she slammed the cupboard door shut!

'All right, what now?' she said.

Neon eyed the cupboard nervously.

'Filly!' Greg spluttered. 'You just put the Gooheads in a cupboard! The rulers of the UNIverse! Stuffed! In a cupboard!'

Filly rolled her eyes. 'They're just heads in goo. Plus, the UHs are about to destroy the

UNIverse and all they can think about is punishing Neon and Moya. No thank you very much.'

'*JUST* HEADS IN GOO?!' came a muffled cry from the cupboard.

Filly sat down on a gooey armchair and bobbed about. 'Who cares who's to blame at this stage? What a waste of precious, precious time! Now, let's make a plan.'

'About five minutes ago all you would talk about was how it was all my fault,' Neon pointed out.

'Yeah,' Filly said. 'Because we were running between locations, so we had some time to point a finger or two. If anything it was actually a really good use of time. The Gooheads don't have time to point fingers.'

'WE DON'T EVEN HAVE FINGERS!' came a muffled shout.

'I'm a little worried you're for the goo pits now,' Greg said to Filly.

'At this stage, we'll either save the UNIverse, in which case they can thank me, or the goo pits won't exist, because the UNIverse won't exist!'

'Good point,' Greg said.

'GREG!' came a disapproving and muffled shout from the cupboard.

He turned nervously to Neon. 'So what's the plan?'

'Me?' Neon said. 'I was going to ask you! You're the one who brought us here, to the Wobbly Under.'

'Ah yes! I almost forgot,' Greg said. He scuttled across the room and pulled at a string of goo dangling from the ceiling. In a flash, the goo began to sparkle, and little scenes began to appear on the floor, walls and ceiling. A melted Goomart, a tiny Priscilla shooting red goo from her eyeballs. A trotting sweet shop bounding up a mountainside, a gooey underwater world filled with sea monsters and kelpies and combs.

'It's … it's … *everything*,' Neon whispered. 'The Wobbly Under is where you can see the entire UNIverse.'

Greg nodded as he prodded a sofa-shaped blob of goo that was now displaying a huge rainbow peppered with houses. 'I haven't even been to the south of the UNIverse – the Rainbow Realm. But here it is!'

Filly rubbed her hands together eagerly. 'We can

draw up a battle plan. We can be one step ahead of the UHs at all times!'

Neon watched as Priscilla tried some outfit goos at the Slimy Wardrobe, her usual pink dress morphing into a big ballgown and then with a *pop* changing to a Goomart apron.

'The Goomart,' Neon said sadly, walking over to the scene and tracing the spot where the Goomart once stood. It had almost completely melted to nothing.

'No time for sentimentality,' Filly said, shoving her aside. 'THIS IS WAR.'

'Filly scares me,' Geldie whispered to Neon.

Suddenly a searing pain shot through Neon's hand.

'Ow!' she cried, doubling over.

'What's wrong?' Moya said, running to her side.

'My hand,' Neon said. 'It's stinging.'

The goo from the pet egg was still on it, but now it had formed a solid layer that she couldn't get off. Like a crusty glove.

'Wait,' Moya said. 'Where did that goo come from?'

'From the pet egg the Whiskers & Gloop guy threw at me.'

Moya's eyes grew wide. 'Neon, you know what this means, don't you?'

'I have absolutely no idea,' Neon said.

'GELDIE!' Moya cried. 'Look at Neon's hand!'

'Oh wow,' Geldie said knowingly. 'A rare one.'

Neon looked to Filly and Greg, but they were busy plotting something in the corner, mumbling words like 'battle' and 'demolish' and 'kaboom'.

'You got the best one!' Moya cried, and Neon was sure she saw Menace Goo Smasher frown.

'Except for you, Menace Goo Smasher!' Moya added.

'The best what?' Neon said, just as the remaining goo in the egg smashed out and began bouncing around the room!

'That'd better not be what I think it is,' Filly said, rushing over and dragging Greg with her.

The goo began to expand, growing bigger and bigger.

'Can we even contain it?' Greg fretted.

'CONTAIN WHAT?' Neon cried. 'WHY DO YOU ALL KNOW WHAT IT IS AND I DON'T?'

Her hand was throbbing. The goo was pulling her towards it.

'WHAT IS HAPPENING?'

Suddenly, a horse burst from the goo! Glorious and golden with a rainbow mane and tail. And a horn.

'It's a Greg unicorn,' Neon said, underwhelmed.

She felt her hand move fast to the horse's mane, like a magnet. Then something incredible happened: huge neon-green wings unfurled from the unicorn's back.

'There it is!' Moya said in awe. 'It's a WINGED unicorn.'

'Another idea of yours?' Neon asked Greg.

'Yes,' Greg said. 'But the Gooheads thought it was too far-fetched, so we went with the wingless one instead.'

'IT WAS TOO FAR-FETCHED,' came a muffled shout from the cupboard.

It nuzzled into Neon, slapping everyone else away with its wings.

'Two gooey Greg unicorns is far too many in the

Wobbly Under,' Filly said. 'This is a war room! Tell them to wait outside.'

'In the dangerous, UH-infested streets? No way,' Moya said, with uncharacteristic anger. But then she added, 'If that's OK, please?'

Neon stared up at the gooey beast in awe. They locked eyes and Neon was positive it gave her a wink. It was the most beautiful thing she had ever seen, and the gooiest.

'You can fly on it, you know,' Geldie said.

'Flying, oh that's brilliant,' Filly said, changing her tune. 'Maybe we can use the Greg unicorns to our advantage. We could attack from the air.'

'What are you going to call him?' Moya asked Neon excitedly.

'Trotty Wonder,' Filly said. 'It's got to be Trotty Wonder.'

Neon looked at the unicorn, and gently stroked his wing. 'No, I was thinking I could call him—'

'It's going to be terrible,' Filly said. 'But you know what, we're at war so call him whatever silly name you want, who cares.'

'I *will*,' Neon said defiantly. 'I hereby name you … Glopglop.'

Filly twitched, struggling to contain her displeasure. But Glopglop stood tall and proud and thankfully not sentient enough to understand his silly name.

17

War and Glopglop

Neon sat in the Wobbly Under watching in horror as the UHs destroyed Lumino. They were growing more and more powerful. More monstrous and deadly. Whiskers & Gloop was now more gloop than whiskers, and the Slimy Wardrobe was more slime than wardrobe, and Glittervoles was less glitter and mostly just voles. Millions of them, scuttling around aimlessly in angry red goo.

Mrs Knackerman and Mr Ragwort walked arm in arm around the square, growling and shooting red goo from their eyes and their fingers and even vomiting it from their mouths. Their eyes were growing bigger and redder, their hair was standing on end.

'They're changing,' Neon said nervously.

'They're monsters,' Geldie said with a shiver. But

then Neon noticed something strange. Priscilla's supply of goo seemed to be slowing down. Now it was only dripping out of her eyes, like a leaky tap.

'SHE'S interesting,' Filly said, leaning over Neon's shoulder with a notepad and pen. 'Who is she?'

'Priscilla Knackerman,' Neon said. 'She's our age. Lives next door to me in the human world. She discovered my secret weeks ago, but didn't tell the other UHs, not until she had stolen the portal opener from me – but even then the UHs didn't believe her.'

Filly scribbled furiously in the notebook. '*She* is the weak link. Look, her UH powers are broken. And we need to figure out why.'

'But why?' Neon asked.

'Isn't it obvious?' Filly said. 'Because if we can figure out why her powers have stopped working properly, we can unlock how to break them all.'

'Oh!' Neon said. 'That's good.'

'But we need to separate her from the group,' Filly said. 'If we can do that, then we can capture her and study her. Tell me everything, I need more information about her to formulate a plan.'

'Um ...' Neon said. 'She ...'

She paused. Neon realised she knew almost nothing about Priscilla. Then she remembered something.

'Oh!' she cried. 'She likes the Spice Girls! They're a human world band.'

'Hmm,' Filly said. 'Are they anything like the Mice Gurls? Could we lure her with them?'

'Maybe,' Neon said. 'They have similar songs. But there's one big difference ... the Spice Girls are not mice.'

'Would she notice?' Filly asked seriously. 'How good is her eyesight?'

'Good enough to tell the difference between a human and a mouse,' Neon said.

Filly nodded. 'Yes, I suppose there's a significant height difference.'

'Yes,' Neon agreed.

'Because the Mice Gurls are ten times the height of a human singer.'

'Yes …' Neon agreed again. 'WAIT, WHAT?!'

'The Mice Gurls are massive,' Geldie said. 'Each one is practically as tall as a building.'

Neon knew she shouldn't have been surprised the superstar singing mice band in the UNIverse was made up of supersized giant mice, but she was.

'But they look so small on the T-shirts and hats their fans wear!' Neon said.

'That's because T-shirts and hats are quite small,' Moya said. 'If someone printed you on a T-shirt, you'd look smaller too.'

'Greg,' Filly said. 'You're famous – how do we get hold of the Mice Gurls?'

Greg walked over and pointed at the wall, to a spot showing a sprawling sparkly city nestled within a glowing mountain. 'They live in the Glow Mountains. Right at the top. But it's too far, we'd never get to them in time.'

Filly turned slowly on her heel. She pointed at Glopglop. 'What if Neon were to *fly*?'

18

The Mice Gurls

'Can't someone else go?' Neon said, wobbling on top of Glopglop, who was himself on top of the roof of Goohead Central. Neon dared to peek over the edge. The force of the wind whipped her hair back and wobbled her cheeks.

'You have to go,' Moya said as she trotted up on Menace Goo Smasher. 'Because Glopglop will only fly for you.'

'Great,' Neon said, gritting her teeth. 'So what exactly is the plan?'

'Fly to the Glow Mountains, find the Mice Gurls, then bring them back to Lumino to lure Priscilla away from the UHs,' Greg said.

'And how will I find them?'

'Five gigantic singing mice?' Filly snorted. 'I think you'll manage.'

Neon held tightly to Glopglop's mane and willed him forwards. She closed her eyes, let out a squeal and –

WHOOSH!

'I'm flying! I'm flying!' Neon cried. 'I hate it!'

Back down on the roof, Menace Goo Smasher reared up excitedly.

'Woah, STOP!' Moya cried, as she realised what he was about to do. 'Yooooou caaaaan't flyyyyyyyyy Mennnnnnnnnaaaaaace Goooooooo Smaaaaasherrrr,' she screamed. But it was too late. Menace Goo Smasher took one wobbly leap and slopped right over the edge.

'No!' Neon cried as she watched Moya fall. She faffed with Glopglop's mane. 'How do I steer *down*? I need to save her.'

'I think it's meant to come naturally or whatever?' Filly shouted up to her. 'But I suppose you are a human.'

'They're heading for the pavement!' Geldie cried, just as there was an almighty

CRUNCH!

They all stared down in shocked silence at the gooey puddle on the pavement.

'Oh dear, that's awful,' Filly said. 'Menace Goo Smasher would've been very useful.'

'And MOYA?!' Neon shouted down.

'She would've been less useful in battle, actually,' Filly said.

'Filly!' Geldie said. 'Stop it!'

Neon stared in disbelief, her eyes welling with tears. Then suddenly, a hand shot up out of the goo puddle. Then an arm, then a face!

'I'm fine!' Moya said, slipping to her feet. She began peeling Menace Goo Smasher off the pavement and squishing him back into shape. 'Menace Goo Smasher is also fine!' She tried to straighten his horn, which was newly shaped like a bolt of lightning, but nothing worked, so she gave up.

'That'll do,' she said, staring at the wonky horn.

'Time to fly, Neon,' Filly said, tapping her watch.

Neon sighed and did what came naturally – she flopped forward on Glopglop and buried her head in his mane. As if by magic that did the trick and they shot off towards the multicoloured lights of the Glow Mountains.

As expected, even in the large expanse of the Glow Mountains, five massive mice who sing pretty much constantly, and with microphones, were relatively easy to find.

It was a lot harder to convince them to come with her to save the UNIverse.

'Why do you think we could help?' the one wearing the baby-blue dress said.

'Yeah,' said the one in leopard-print leggings. 'We're just mice.'

'Singing mice,' said the one in a little black miniskirt.

'MASSIVE singing mice!' roared the one in a sports cap, as she did a high kick.

'Well,' Neon said, 'essentially, one of the UHs is a big fan of the Spice Girls in the human world, and I think you're strangely similar and could possibly lure her away from the pack.'

'What kind of songs do the Spice Girls sing?'

Neon wiggled uncomfortably on Glopglop. In the distance she could see Lumino melting under lava-like goo.

'Oh, well,' she said, feeling she had no option but to launch into song.

One of the mice handed her a microphone.

'Oh no,' she said, 'that's not—'

'SING!' they said, forcing Neon to sing a few more lines. They boomed out loudly all around her and someone nearby shouted, 'PUT A SOCK IN IT!'

'See?' Neon said. 'Doesn't it remind you of your "If You Wanna Be My Cheese" song?'

The mice all exchanged glances.

'No,' the one in the black skirt finally said. 'It doesn't even have cheese in it. And cheese is the best ingredient for a song. But anyway, not the point. We're NOT coming with you. Not down there – not to *that* UH-infested mess.'

Neon began biting her nails. She was sure she could hear the screaming drifting up from Lumino. What was she going to do? She couldn't return without the Mice Gurls! It was such a huge part of the plan! It was currently the *only* part of the plan!

'Um, well, there is another *really good* reason to come to Lumino,' Neon lied. 'Could you just move a *smidge* closer.'

19

Jerry Leaves the Band

'She's back!' Moya cheered from the roof of Goohead Central as Neon soared towards them, dangling over Glopglop's side, holding up a string of five giant struggling mice.

'Subtle,' Filly said, rolling her eyes. 'She couldn't have used a shrink goo or a hide and vanish goo. No, she decided to just fly the giant mice over the city.'

There was a rumble of feet, followed by screams of joy.

'THE MICE GURLS!'

'Oh no,' Geldie whispered, as they watched crowds of unicorns burst from their hiding places and charge towards Goohead Central.

Just behind them, the UHs began sniffing madly, their eyes glowing bright.

'Is the plan working?' Neon puffed.

'NO!' Filly cried. 'Neon, what have you done?!'

'We meant bring them back *subtly*,' Filly said, as they cowered on the roof with five giant famous mice, all itching to sing.

'Subtly?' Neon scoffed. 'Look at them!'

'Neon, you work at the Goomart, surely you know by now to use some goos to help? Now we have a disaster on our hands – the Mice Gurls have lured hundreds of unicorns out of hiding and they're all going to be annihilated by the UHs –' she peered over the edge – 'WHO ARE ON THEIR WAY!'

'Go home!' Neon hissed to the crowd. 'Save yourselves!'

'They're superfans, that won't work,' Geldie said.

'They'd risk being zapped by UHs just to see their favourite band?' Neon cried.

'Well, yes,' Geldie said. 'Because they're superfans.'

Filly began pacing. Neon could see the defeat in her eyes and she didn't like it.

'You were going to distract Priscilla with the Mice Gurls,' Neon said. 'Well, what if we split the Mice Gurls – I'll use one of them to lure the crowd away to safety, and you can all take the rest to Priscilla.'

Filly looked up. 'That might work.'

So Neon leaped on to Glopglop and grabbed one of the giant mice, the one with ginger hair. 'Sorry about this, but we need to make another quick trip.'

She flew up high into the air, the giant mouse dangling for the crowd to see.

'LOOK!' a unicorn in the crowd cried, pointing

madly in the air. 'The Mice Gurls are leaving!'

'OH MY UNICORNS, IT'S JUST JERRY! HAS JERRY LEFT THE BAND?! WE LOVE YOU, JERRY! COME BACK, JERRY!' The wild crowd began charging through the streets after Neon, their arms raised as they tried to grab the famous mouse.

Neon looked back to see Filly tipping some goo over the rest of the mice, and with a fizzle they shrank, smaller and smaller until Filly could fit all four in her pocket.

'Why didn't I think of that?' Neon groaned.

'WHAT?' Jerry shouted up.

'Nothing!' Neon replied, as the crowds of superfan unicorns galloped along the road nicely beneath them. 'Everything is going to plan.'

'Maybe we should do a song to celebrate,' Jerry said.

'That's not necessary right now,' Neon insisted, but Jerry wasn't listening and launched into a rendition of their hit 'If You Wanna Be My Cheese'.

* * *

Back at Goohead Central, Filly was already on the street, ducking and diving down alleyways with the now shrunken mice in her palm.

'You shrank us!' the leopard-print one shouted.

'Yeah, sorry about that,' Filly said. 'It was a cheap shrink goo though, so it'll probably only last a few minutes. Which means we have to be quick.'

Filly spied Priscilla in the procession of UHs making their way across town. She ducked as some red goo shot over her head, then she rolled into a doorway.

'First that girl takes us from the Glow Mountains—'

Filly looked down at the mice. 'Neon didn't explain the plan?'

'Sort of, but we said no – then she grabbed Sporty Mouse's leg and hoisted her in the air, so Baby Mouse grabbed hold to try to get her back, but that flying goo unicorn is strong, so she went up in the air, and then Posh Mouse grabbed on to her, and, well, you get the idea. Soon we were a string of mice flying through the air!'

155

Filly shook her head. 'I apologise on behalf of my friend, she's a human.'

'Ah,' the mice said knowingly.

Footsteps got closer. Filly held a finger to her mouth to silence the mice. The UHs were filing past the doorway, grunting and growling like wild animals. They had reached the next stage of UH-evolution and were now multiplying. In mere minutes they had gone from twenty to two hundred. At the very back of the ever expanding pack was Priscilla, who was still unimpressively dribbling goo from her eyeballs.

'I think that UH is broken,' one of the mice whispered.

Filly nodded. 'Exactly. And that is why she's interesting. We need her in order to understand how UHs work, and how they can be defeated. Please would you jump on her shoulder and sing a song quietly in her ear? I need to distract her enough to separate her from her friends.'

The mice sprang into action, bouncing effortlessly over the gooey puddles of red goo and landing on Priscilla's shoulder. And then they began to sing.

Priscilla stopped dead in her tracks.

Filly peeked out. The other UHs were marching on, but Priscilla was transfixed. Frozen to the spot. She began to sway.

Quickly, Filly pulled a small pot of goo from her pocket and threw it, hitting Priscilla square in the face.

Then came an almighty *SPLASH* – the goo engulfed Priscilla and she and the mice completely vanished into the gloop!

Filly checked the coast was clear and then she scooped the goo back into the jar and scurried off to meet the others at Goohead Central.

'YOU SENT US TO THE SWIMMING POOL OF DOOM!' the mouse in the little blue dress cried as the mice emerged from the goo and grew back to their usual large size. They balled their fists and shook them angrily in Filly's direction.

'I've got a limited number of goos on me,' Filly explained. 'It was the only transportation goo I had, and I needed to trap Priscilla somewhere to carry her back here.'

'Do you KNOW what is in the Swimming Pool of Doom?' the mouse in the sports cap shouted.

'Oh-oh-oh!' Moya said, raising her hand. 'I went once as a dare at a sleepover. There were sharks and, weirdly, an orchestra of lobsters playing sinister music with their pincers.'

'Well, today,' the mouse in the black skirt said

pointedly, 'it was a CAT CONVENTION. And do you know what cats hate? WATER. So they drained the Swimming Pool of Doom, so instead of goo and water in it, we fell into a pool ENTIRELY FULL OF CATS.'

'I would've LOVED that, but probably because cats don't want to eat me,' Moya said.

In the distance, Neon was herding the superfans into an empty building. On the ground, Geldie was waiting, ready to bolt the door.

There was a *CLANG!*

'They're in!' Geldie cheered, signalling for Neon to head back to Goohead Central.

Neon could see the streams of glowing red goo trailing through the city. The shrieks had died down and now all that could be heard was the whistling of the wind and the thundering rumble of the advancing UHs. Neon knew where they were heading. If they wanted to destroy the UNIverse they'd have to destroy its rulers. They were heading for Goohead Central.

Neon left Jerry on the roof, discussing the horrors of the Swimming Pool of Doom goo with the other Mice Gurls. She promised to take them home as soon as they'd defeated the UHs, then clattered back downstairs and slipped through the secret Greg entrance to the Wobbly Under.

Inside, Filly was prodding Priscilla, who was standing very still, her red glowing eyes staring blankly ahead.

'HAVE YOU GOT AN UH IN HERE?' came a cry from the Gooheads in the cupboard. 'WE SENSE ONE!'

'I DO NOT!' Filly lied.

When Priscilla saw Neon, the sinister red glow of her eyes dulled.

'Neon Gallup!' she cried, immediately followed by, 'I WILL DESTROY ALL THE UNICORNS!'

'Interesting,' Filly said. 'She's a monster now, but her human world version is still there – look, she recognised you.'

160

Red goo dribbled from Priscilla's mouth.

'Ew,' Geldie said.

'Do you think her evil transformation isn't quite working because she actually likes me?' Neon said.

Filly narrowed her eyes. 'This is not a fairytale, Neon – this is real life! No, it's something much more interesting than that. I think she's been contaminated and it's affecting her ability to morph into a fully evil UH.'

'Contaminated with what?' Neon asked.

'It must be something very powerful. Think, Neon,' Filly said, weaving closer until they were practically nose to nose. 'Has Priscilla come into contact with anything from the UNIverse that the others haven't?'

'I haven't really been watching her since she got here,' Neon said. 'Maybe the Swimming Pool of Doom?'

'Nah, that's not it,' Filly said. 'She was malfunctioning before I sent her there.'

Moya gasped. Her eyes were wide. 'Neon,' she said excitedly. 'She put the lipstick on.'

'What?' Filly said, her face brightening. 'The portal opener?'

'WHAT?!' cried the Gooheads from the cupboard. Neon could hear spluttering and words like 'irresponsible' and 'human nightmare'.

'Priscilla stole the portal opener,' Neon confirmed, 'and then she put it on her lips.'

Filly began bouncing on the spot. The others joined in. The fact they were in the Wobbly Under meant their heads were bouncing off the ceiling.

Priscilla stood in the middle of it all, looking under-whelmed and still mildly evil.

'What is it?' Neon asked. 'What's so exciting?'

'That's got to be it!' Filly said, clicking her fingers for Neon to hand over the lipstick. She smeared a little more on Priscilla's lips and watched as the UH licked it. Immediately the red goo dried up a bit more!

'That's how we break them!' Moya cheered. 'We're sort of weaponising a makeover!'

Suddenly, a *BANG* sounded outside.

'They're here,' Greg said shakily. 'It's the UHs!'

Filly threw open the doors to the cupboard. Four

162

furious Gooheads bobbed in their jars. Neon felt their eyes on her.

'Let an UH get hold of the portal opener and put it on like make-up,' the purple head tutted.

'Yeah, yeah, get over it,' Filly said, reaching into the cupboard to grab them. 'Your services are required to save the UNIverse, so you're coming with us.'

'We're the rulers of the UNIverse, Filly Spangle. Stop bossing us about!' the blue head bellowed. 'What do you want us to do?'

'Make some more portal opener lipsticks,' Filly said with a smile.

'Absolutely not!' the purple head yelled.

'Out of the question!' the green head said. 'And anyway, even if we agreed, we need the right goo brewing location – it would have to be spotlessly clean, for starters, and this place is full of Greg unicorn poo.'

Moya looked sheepishly at the floor. 'Menace Goo Smasher has had a scary day, it's not his fault.'

'I know just the place,' Filly said. 'Come on.'

20

Twizzle Again

'NO, ABSOLUTELY NOT! GO AWAY! I'M IN HIDING! THERE ARE UHS ON THE LOOSE!! AND I'D NEVER HELP YOU AFTER WHAT YOU ALL DID!'

They were all huddled outside the Grand Twizzle restaurant. It was a tall building with a curled roof, just like Twizzle's moustache. The shutters were down and the door was bolted, and Twizzle had made it clear from the other side that they were not coming in and absolutely under no circumstances were they brewing goo in his spotless kitchen. After all, they had accused him of being a secret UH!

'Oh come on, Twizzle,' Neon shouted through the door. 'You were only captured temporarily! You were barely interrogated.'

'Old Lady Buck was threatening to use terrible goos on me!' he cried.

Her name made Neon's stomach sink. She wanted more than anything to race to the Goomart and check if she was all right. But first she had to save the UNIverse …

'You stole me away and said I was the Long-Lost Unicorn Hunter!' Twizzle reminded them. 'And it was GREG.'

Greg shrugged. 'I'm as shocked as anyone. It was news to me!'

A hatch in the door snapped open and Twizzle peered out.

'And is that an UH you've brought to my restaurant?' he cried at the sight of Priscilla.

'Yes,' Filly said, stepping forward. 'She's helped us figure out how to save the UNIverse.'

'Oh enough of the chit-chat. Open up, Twizzle, you old saucepan,' came a voice.

The others moved to reveal the Gooheads.

'Your Gooeynesses!' Twizzle said. 'To what do I owe the pleasure?'

A huge *BANG* sounded behind them, followed by unicorns screaming. In the distance, buildings slopped to the ground.

'UHs are melting the city as we speak, and these young unicorns have figured out how to stop them,' the purple head said. 'So let us in, will you? And quickly.'

Neon stared, open-mouthed, as the Gooheads' newly made goo stretched from jar to jar, glowing and cracking in Twizzle's sparkling kitchen. It was unlike any goo she had seen before. In it was every colour of the rainbow, gushing through veinlike strands.

'Wow,' she whispered in awe, just as a neat little string of lipsticks exactly like hers popped from the goo.

'Made in the same way as the original,' Filly said, plucking a lipstick from the goo with fascination. 'So these should have the same effect on the others as yours did on Priscilla, Neon.'

'LET'S HOPE SO,' the purple head said. 'Take one, each of you. And once you've used them, I want them to be returned IMMEDIATELY for destruction.'

'Must she be here?' Twizzle asked, pointing at Priscilla as the tiniest dribble of red goo slipped from her mouth. 'She's putting me off.' But no one was listening to him.

'It's a little like the old days, isn't it?' the yellow head said.

'Yes,' the green head said. 'Exhausting. I hate brewing goo.'

'How did you end up with your heads in jars?' Neon dared to ask. 'Did the unicorns rebel and cut off your heads and you were saved by someone and kept alive in your jars?'

That's always what Neon had imagined must've happened.

The Gooheads looked confused.

'We were born this way,' the blue head said.

'With your head in a jar?' Neon scoffed.

The Gooheads nodded and Neon realised they weren't joking.

'Oh,' she said. 'That's weird …'

'We were born to brew goo, but as the UNIverse grew,' the purple head went on, 'it became too much for four heads in goo to make all the goo for everyone, so we built factories to make them quickly, and much more cheaply – the Goomart opened up and the rest is history. And then we turned our attention to ruling everything instead of goo brewing. Much less work.'

'We oversee all goo brewing, of course,' the blue head said. 'Well, aside from the stuff brewed by the dreadful Strange Goo Society. Theirs is unregulated goo brewing and we're always trying to find them!'

Filly, Twizzle and Neon all exchanged glances.

A much-needed *BANG* from outside broke the silence.

Filly's face darkened. 'Now comes the hard part.'

21

Showdown

Neon and the others crept along the streets, scuttling from doorway to doorway in search of UHs.

They heard a rustle, the sound of pounding shoes on the pavement.

Neon dared to look.

'Is it the UHs?!' Geldie fretted. 'We're not ready!'

In the distance, the UHs howled like hyper wolves. Their shouts were getting closer. Up above their heads, Neon could see the skyline falling as red goo consumed buildings.

'RUN!' a unicorn cried as he tore past. 'They're coming this way!'

Trembling, Neon jumped on to Glopglop.

Filly brandished her lipstick. 'Now we save the UNIverse.'

'Where am I?' came a whimper. Priscilla was looking up and down the street, her eyes filled with fear.

'Sssh,' Neon begged as Filly raced over and put a hand over Priscilla's mouth.

'You're in the UNIverse,' Filly explained. 'Your UH-ness has been waning for some time now and you're almost back to boring human.'

'What?' Priscilla screamed.

'Moya,' Filly said, taking her hand from Priscilla's mouth and wiping it on her dress. 'Distract her, you're better at comforting people.'

'*Well*,' Moya said in a panic as she took off her boots and handed them to Priscilla. 'What you're holding in your hand is a pair of Greg unicorn boots. I made them myself – you can add a horn and a mane to anything and make it look like a Greg unicorn.'

'Neon,' Priscilla said. 'What's happening!?'

'I'll explain later,' Neon said, ruffling Glopglop's mane and taking off into the sky. 'I've got a UNIverse to save!'

Filly plonked Moya's woolly unicorn hat on Priscilla.

'You wait here with the Gooheads, we'll be back.'

'The Goo ... whats?' Priscilla whimpered, as Filly hastily wheeled the Gooheads up to her.

'First they locked us in the cupboard and *now* we're being left with a malfunctioning UH,' the purple head complained as he *smooshed* his nose against the glass to get a better look at Priscilla. 'Fascinating beast, the UH.'

Priscilla SCREAMED!

High up in the purple and gold clouds, Neon watched the others run off down the street – armed with their lipsticks – before breaking off in different directions. Among the melted buildings and fleeing unicorns she could see the UHs. They were larger now, with goo spikes running from the top of their heads all the way down their backs. Their fingers had grown longer, and their eyes were so large and red she could feel the searing heat of their stares from all the way up in the clouds. Their monstrous transformation looked almost complete.

The plan was to surround them, then dart among their ranks smearing them with the lipstick. Neon would attack from the air once the ground cavalry had gone in, and she'd pick off any that were proving difficult to catch on foot.

Neon felt her palms getting sweaty. She wobbled about in the clouds to the sound of muffled screams and falling buildings below her. She could just fly off, she thought … Maybe she could go and befriend the kelpies in Lumino Falls and hide there forever with a face covered in fish. Or she could fly to Mystica! That sounded like a fun place. Ooh, or the Glow Mountains where she picked up the Mice Gurls …

'NEON!' came a mouse shout. She spun round to see the Mice Gurls huddled on top of a building and pointing madly beyond her. 'Your friends need you!'

Below, Neon could see the attack had been launched. Lipstick was being smeared on UHs, red goo was flying. She hunched over, sending Glopglop into a spectacular nosedive.

Down they went, the cold air hitting her cheeks like

173

daggers. Shots of red goo flew past her face as she ducked and weaved and swooped, catching the UHs with her lipstick.

'It's working!' came Filly's delighted shout from the crowd. 'Keep going!'

But it was all too much for Glopglop. The flying unicorn reared and bucked and shook in the air and started to veer off course.

'Steady! Steady!' Neon pleaded.

Greg, Geldie and Filly were busily running circles around the UHs, smearing lipstick on their lips with impressive efficiency. The UHs seemed so confused by the attack that they had become virtually motionless.

Mr Ragwort's bright red eyes began to fade. The spikes on his back wilted. The spray of goo coming from his mouth collapsed to the ground.

'Almost there!' Neon cried, scanning the crowd. Nearly all of them were malfunctioning now. Their duplicates were melting. All the red goo splattered around town began to crisp up and turn to dust.

But then Neon heard a strange groaning noise. Behind her and caked in goo, Goohead Central began to wobble.

'The building is going to fall!' Neon cried, the panic rising in her fast. 'Get out of the way!'

But her friends couldn't hear her, the winds were too strong, she was too high up. She'd never reach them in time!

She flew around the building, steering Glopglop as close as she could, then pressed her hands against it as if that might hold it upright. The goo stung and made the coloured stripe in her hair burn. It was no good. The building gave a final groan and began to slop forward. Glopglop tore off as the gloopy building began to collapse towards them.

'The building! The goo! The building! IT'S FALLING!' Neon bellowed.

But it was no good, her friends on the ground were too distracted!

'LOOK UP!' Neon begged. 'AND THEN RUN AWAY! OR JUST RUN AWAY WITHOUT LOOKING!'

The building curved over Neon and Glopglop like a mean wave. She was so close to her friends. The building was so close to them too.

'RUN!' Neon screamed.

Her friends looked up just as Glopglop shot out from under the building, carrying Neon to safety.

The last thing she saw was their terrified faces as the building crashed down, burying them – and the UHs – under a mountain of goo.

Neon guided Glopglop in to land and dismounted before his hoofs had hit the ground.

'FILLY!' she cried, racing to the scene. 'GELDIE! GREG!'

Nothing.

She fell to her knees.

'Filly,' she sobbed. 'Geldie, Greg …'

She'd finally done it. She'd killed them all. It was over. She had destroyed lives and an entire magical world!

'I'M A MONSTER!' she wailed.

Squelch.

Neon looked up hopefully.

Squelch.

Her face brightened. Was that—? Yes! One by one, like kelpies breaking the surface of the lagoon, her friends emerged, limb by limb, from the thick goo!

'YOU'RE OK!' Neon cheered, leaping to her feet and scooping them into a hug.

'We got them all!' Filly said with uncharacteristic excitement.

Slowly, the UHs emerged from the goo too. Their powers had been reduced to almost nothing, their eyes were flickering back to normal, and the red goo from their mouths was mere dribble.

'I got that one, and that one and that one,' Filly said, pointing at each of them.

But then something strange happened. Beneath the goo came a red light. It pulsed and danced and broke through the surface.

It was Mrs Knackerman and she was *glowing.* And not in a good way.

'Um,' Neon said. 'Did someone forget Mrs Knackerman?'

'UNICORNS,' she seethed, firing red goo at Neon.

Neon dodged the goo.

'We forgot Mrs Knackerman!' she cried. She knew now that even one UH was a problem if they could multiply! She fumbled around desperately in her pocket for her lipstick.

'Got it!' she cried, holding it aloft, but Mrs Knackerman sent a spray of red goo right at it and knocked it from her grasp.

'Should've seen that coming,' Neon groaned.

'Neon!' Filly screamed. 'She's going to grab the lipstick!'

Neon watched in horror as Mrs Knackerman stomped towards the portal opener.

'NOT TODAY, MRS KNACKERMAN!' Neon cried, leaping to her feet and running as fast as she could. She was running faster than she had ever run before. Her heart felt like it was pounding in her eyeballs, she couldn't breathe. Her little legs were going like the clappers. She was going to get there first, she was going to get the lip—

SMACK!

Something hit Neon hard in the chest and everything went black.

When she came to, the world was hazy. A familiar shape slowly formed in front of her. The thing that had knocked her sideways.

'You have *got* to be kidding,' she said, as the trotting sweet shop of Mystica pranced from foot to foot in front of her.

'NEON!' Geldie, Moya and Filly cried at once. 'BEHIND YOU!'

Neon turned to see Mrs Knackerman had abandoned her attempt to get the lipstick and had instead decided to eat her. She loomed over her, her spiky goo-stained gnashers open wide.

But just as Neon was beginning to think all hope was lost, a shadow darted about in the distance beyond. They picked up the lipstick and slowly began to creep forward.

'EAT THE UNICORN!' Mrs Knackerman roared and was about to crunch! But a hand got there first – a hand holding a lipstick! The green goo seeped into Mrs Knackerman's teeth and instantly she grew smaller, and less red, and a lot less spiky.

'You did it!' Neon cheered, craning her neck to see who it was.

Standing there, with his chin thrust proudly in the air, was Greg.

'Did I just save the UNIverse *again*?' he said. 'I think I just did.'

Geldie hung his head. 'He's going to be insufferable now.'

THE GLOOPY

*Lumino's No. 1 mag, where goo
and style collide!*

SKY-HIGH
INSPIRATION!

Did you spot our favourite humicorn, Neon Gallup, soaring through the skies with the Mice Gurls? What a sight to see two of *The Gloopy*'s favourite style inspirations joining forces! If you too want to join the fun, follow these simple steps:

1. Get your mouse ears out and dress like a giant superstar mouse.

You can choose which member of the band you most want to dress like!

2. Add a nod to our favourite humicorn with some tie-dye tights.

3. Sing 'If You Wanna Be My Cheese'.

4. Save the UNIverse!

22

Through the Portal

Neon opened a portal to the human world on the pavement outside what remained of Glittervoles, and nodded her thanks to the off cheeses in platform shoes who had helped them round up the UHs.

The Gooheads bobbed in their goo jars and smiled.

'The UNIverse is saved!' Greg said grandly. 'Thanks to ME!'

Priscilla was standing by the swirling portal, lost in thought.

'I'm sorry, Neon,' she said quietly. 'It's not so bad here, and unicorns aren't so bad either.'

Neon patted her on the back. 'Oh, Priscilla, I wish you could stay and see the sights. It's so much fun. I could take you to Glittervoles for a Volefizz. Suzette owns the place, she's a squirrel made of sprinkles. Yeah,

I can tell by your face maybe that's one weird thing too many for a single day. But it's really magical here – and I've only explored a small part of it so far.'

'And you will be exploring no more,' the Gooheads said. 'Neon, you will give us the portal opener and go home with the UHs. AND YOU WILL NEVER RETURN.'

Neon's heart sank faster than a goo canoe being attacked by kelpies.

But as much as it stung, and was the worst thing to happen to her, she knew it was only fair. After all, the whole mess was her fault.

'It's the right thing,' Neon said, readying to drop the lipstick into the purple Goohead's jar. 'I'll leave—'

'Not so fast!' interrupted a voice, and much to Neon's astonishment out of the rubble marched Old Lady Buck! Suzette bounced along by her feet.

'I thought you were making up the squirrel made of sprinkles!' Priscilla cried with delight. 'It's real! IT'S AMAZING!'

Suzette raised her paws and batted the praise away. 'Oh stop it!' she chuckled. 'Stop it!'

Neon wasn't listening. 'Old Lady Buck,' she said in disbelief. 'You're here? You're OK!'

'Suzette found me and gave me some Volefizz and now I'm as good as new! As that famous saying goes, you can always count on a squirrel made of sprinkles.'

She stood squarely in front of the Gooheads. 'You will not banish Neon, she is the BEST goo seller I have ever had at the Goomart. There is not a spill she cannot clean up, or a speciality comb she cannot find.'

'Wait a second …' Filly began, but thought better of finishing.

'If you banish Neon, well, I will close down the Goomart and leave here myself,' Old Lady Buck threatened. 'Maybe I'll retire to the Glow Mountains. You Gooheads will need to go back into goo production, because everyone knows I handle most of that these days. You'd be back doing all the hard work.'

The Gooheads looked worried.

'Fine, *fine*,' the green Goohead said. 'She can stay.'

'Thank you!' Neon mimed to Old Lady Buck, who gave her a wink in return.

'BUT,' the purple Goohead said, 'if she reveals our secret ONE MORE TIME, then that's it. Do you know how much memory goo it's going to take to properly deal with all these UHs?'

'Of course,' Old Lady Buck said, plonking a shopping basket full of jars down in front of them. 'Exactly this amount.' Then Old Lady Buck read the label aloud.

MEMORY-ERASING GOO

Wipe those memories away! Warning: to be used on someone only once. If more than one memory-erasing goo is applied to a person, it will cause some unwanted side effects. These may include: seeing rainbows, sporadic dancing and randomly saying the name of the person who used the previous memory-erasing goo on them.

'You can't erase our memories!' Mrs Knackerman cried.

'We're not, it's technically the goo doing that,'

Suzette said. 'And it'll only erase UNIverse-related memories, don't you worry.'

'I don't want to forget a squirrel made of sprinkles!' Priscilla wailed.

Suzette held her hand to her heart. 'Gosh, maybe I could visit the adoring human in her sleep?'

'NO!' Neon cried. 'That would be *terrifying*.'

'Get to work, unicorns!' Old Lady Buck cheered, throwing them the jars.

One by one, Moya, Filly and Geldie poured the goo on to the UHs' heads. And one by one, Greg ushered them through the portal back to the human world.

Neon breathed a sigh of relief as she watched Mr Ragwort go, followed by Priscilla and then Mrs Knackerman.

'Goodbye, Mrs Knackerman,' Neon said.

'Betye,' Mrs Knackerman replied.

Neon froze.

'What did you say?' she whispered, but Mrs Knackerman turned towards the portal and, with a blank stare, walked through.

'I don't know that human word,' Moya said. 'What does it mean? Betye?'

Neon grabbed her arm and pulled her to the side.

'That's them all!' Greg cried. 'I have saved the UNIverse again!'

Cheers rang out around them and gooey fireworks exploded in the sky. The Mice Gurls' music began to play. But Neon wasn't feeling joyful. She was confused.

'Neon?' Moya whispered. 'What's wrong?'

'Betye,' Neon said quietly, 'is my mum's name. Is it possible *my mum* has used a memory-erasing goo on Mrs Knackerman? The label – it says if you use it more than once it can cause unwanted side effects, including randomly saying the name of the person who used the previous memory-erasing goo on you.'

'But that would mean …' Moya said slowly.

Neon nodded. 'That I'm not the only one with a secret.'

There is a world where witches live, deep down below the sink pipes ...

Read on for a sneak peek at the first book in Sibéal Pounder's Witch Wars series

AVAILABLE NOW!

Prologue

For as long as anyone can remember, witches have lurked on this planet. They have brewed gloopy potions in their cauldrons and torn through the sky on their brooms. They have cackled. They have cursed. They have cats.

Most people think witches are really evil, with their tattered black dresses, pointy hats and unfortunate noses, but that's mostly nonsense and really only half the story. The truth, if you happen to be looking for it, lies deep down below the sink pipes ...

Down the Plughole

It would have been very difficult to spot Fran the fairy on the day this story begins. Her dress may have been puffy, her hair may have been huge, but she was barely the size of a small potato.

Fran was slowly sidestepping across a garden lawn, holding a large, limp leaf in front of her. She didn't want the owner of the garden to see her because Miss Heks was a terrible old woman with a grim face and size eleven shoes. If she had seen Fran she would've squashed her immediately.

Fran and her leaf were on a mission. There was something very important in the shed at the bottom of Miss Heks's garden. That something was a girl called Tiga Whicabim.

'You!' Tiga said, pointing at a slug that was sliding its way across an old stone sink. 'You will be the star of my show! You will play the role of Beryl, an ambitious dancer with severe hiccups.'

Tiga had been in the shed for hours. The evil Miss Heks had been her guardian for as long as Tiga could remember and she had quickly learned to keep out of her way. If she didn't, the old bat would make her sew up the holes in her disgusting, scratchy dresses. Or she would force Tiga to run up and down the garden in her gigantic, ugly shoes, bellowing things like 'FASTER!' and 'OH, DID YOU TRIP?' from the kitchen window.

Tiga shone a torch on the slug.

'You are going to be the best actor the world has ever seen!' she cried.

Fran sighed when she saw that.

Not because she'd finally found Tiga, after a long and perilous journey that had almost ended with her being eaten by a dog.

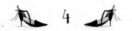

4

No, the reason Fran sighed was because she loved a bit of acting!

Despite her small size, Fran was a big deal in the world of show business. Everyone called her Fran the Fabulous Fairy (a name she had made up for herself). She had hosted many award-winning TV shows like *Cooking for Tiny People* and *The Squashed and the Swatted* and she'd played the lead role in *Glittery Sue* – a tragic drama about a small lady called Sue who got some glitter in her hair and couldn't get it out again.

'An actor you say!' Fran said, making Tiga jump.

Tiga stared, mouth open, at the small person that marched across the shed and – very ungracefully, and with much grunting – climbed up the leg of her trusty old rocking chair.

Fran stretched out a hand.

'Very delighted to meet you, Tiga! Now, it's pronounced *Teega*, isn't it? That's what I thought! I'm very good at names and absolutely everything else. I'm Fran the Fabulous Fairy. But you can call me Fran. Or Fabulous. BUT NEVER JUST FAIRY. I hate that.'

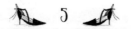

Tiga, understandably, assumed she had gone mad. Or at the very least fallen asleep.

She squinted at the little thing with big hair and then looked to the slug for reassurance, but it was sliding its way across the floor as if it knew exactly who Fran was, and was trying to escape.

'I don't think,' Fran said, pointing at the slug, 'that she should be acting in the lead role. She is slimy and not paying much attention.'

Fran wiggled a foot and a beehive of hair just like her own appeared on top of the slug's head.

'Much, much, *much* better,' she said.

Tiga panicked – the slug had *hair*! Not any old hair, a beehive of perfectly groomed hair! It was a split-second reaction, but with a flick of her hand she batted the fairy clean off the rocking chair.

Fran wobbled from left to right and tried to steady herself.

'Did you just *swat* me?' she snapped. 'The ultimate insult!'

Tiga tried to avoid eye contact and instead looked at

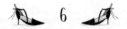

the slug. She couldn't be sure, but it looked a lot like it was shaking its head at her.

'WITCHES ARE NOT ALLOWED TO SWAT FAIRIES. IT IS THE LAW,' Fran ranted.

'I'm sorry!' Tiga cried. 'I didn't think you were real – I thought you were just my imagination! You don't need to call me a witch.'

'Yes I do,' said Fran, floating in front of Tiga with her hands on her hips. 'Because you are one.'

'I am one what?' Tiga asked.

'One witch,' said Fran as she twirled in the air, got her puffy dress caught in her wings and crash-landed on the floor.

'BRAAAAT!' came a bellow from across the garden. 'Time to leave the shed. Your dinner is ready!'

Tiga glanced nervously out of the window. 'If you are real, although I'm still not convinced you are, you'd better leave now. Miss Heks is a terrible old woman and she will do horrible, nasty, ear-pinching things to you.'

Fran ignored her and went back to twirling in the air. 'What are you having for dinner?'

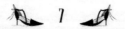

'Cheese water,' Tiga said with a sigh. 'It's only ever cheese water.'

Fran thought about this for a moment. 'And how do you make this cheese water?'

'You find a bit of mouldy old cheese and you put it in some boiling water,' said Tiga, looking ill.

Fran swooped down lower and landed on the sink. 'Well, I'm afraid we don't have cheese water in Ritzy City – it's mostly cakes.'

Tiga stared at the fairy. 'Ritzy where?'

'*Riiiitzzzzzy Ciiiiity!*' Fran cheered, waving her hands in the air.

Tiga shrugged. 'Never heard of it.'

'But you're a witch,' said Fran.

'I am not a witch!' Tiga cried.

'You SO are!'

'I am not!'

'Definitely are,' said Fran, nodding her head. 'Even your name says so.'

And with that she flicked her tiny finger, sending a burst of glittery dust sailing across the room.

8

TIGA WHICABIM, the dust read.

Then it began to wobble and rearrange itself into something new.

I AM A BIG WITCH.

'You've cheated somehow,' Tiga mumbled, moving the dust letters about in the air. Most people would've believed Fran by this point, but Tiga wasn't used to magic and fun and insane fairies. So, despite this very

convincing evidence that she might just be a witch, Tiga still walked towards the door. Towards the cheese water.

'TIGA!' bellowed Miss Heks. 'YOUR CHEESE WATER HAS REACHED BOILING POINT.'

'Cheese water,' Fran chuckled. 'Wait! Where are you going, Tiga?'

'To eat dinner,' said Tiga. 'Bye, Fabulous Fairy Fran. It was lovely to meet you.'

Fran raised a hand in the air. 'Wait! *What?* You're not coming with me to Ritzy City, a place of wonder and absolutely no cheese?'

Tiga paused. Even if it was a mad dream, it was better than cheese water. She turned on her heel and walked back towards Fran.

Fran squealed and squeaked and did somersaults in the air.

'WHAT'S GOING ON IN THERE? I KNOW YOU CAN HEAR ME, YOU LITTLE MAGGOT!' Miss Heks shouted.

Tiga could see Miss Heks stomping her way towards the shed.

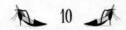

'Quick!' Fran cried. 'We must go to Ritzy City right now!'

'*How?*' Tiga cried, frantically looking around the shed for an escape route.

'Down the sink pipes, of course,' Fran said as she shot through the air and straight down the plughole.

'Come on, Tiga!' her shrill little voice echoed from somewhere inside the sink.

Tiga leaned over the stone sink and stared down the plughole.

There was nothing down there. No light. And certainly no city, that was for sure.

The door to the shed flew open and splinters of old wood went soaring through the air.

'WHAT IS GOING ON?' Miss Heks bellowed.

'NOW!' Fran yelled.

Tiga wiggled a finger in the plughole.

This is nonsense, she thought, just as she disappeared.

WITCH WARS

Read the whole ritzy, glitzy, witchy series!

AVAILABLE NOW!

BAD Mermaids

SIBÉAL POUNDER

BAD Mermaids

Illustrated by Jason Cockcroft

SIBÉAL POUNDER

BAD Mermaids

On the Rocks

Illustrated by Jason Cockcroft

Read the whole fabulously fishy series!

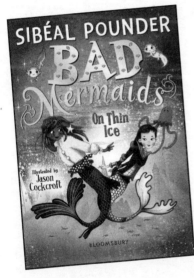

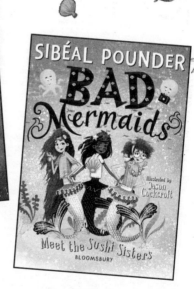

AVAILABLE NOW!

And have you read

What if somewhere along the way we've all got the
Santa story a bit wrong … ?

A funny, festive sleigh ride you'll never forget!

About the Author

Sibéal Pounder is the author of the much-loved and highly successful children's fiction series Witch Wars and Bad Mermaids, and *Tinsel*, a funny feminist play on the Father Christmas story. Before becoming a full-time writer, she researched and wrote for the *Financial Times*. Her first book, *Witch Wars*, was shortlisted for the Waterstones Children's Book Prize and the Sainsbury's Children's Book Award and she was also a World Book Day author in 2019. *Neon and the Unicorn Hunters* is her second goo-tastic tale about Neon Gallup in the extraordinary UNIverse.

About the Illustrator

Sarah Warburton grew up in Anglesey, North Wales, but after studying Illustration at the University of the West of England, she made Bristol her home. She is an internationally acclaimed picture-book illustrator, with titles including *Peter Pan* and the Princess series with Caryl Hart, as well as *The Don't Panic Gang!* with Mark Sperring. Sarah has also illustrated *Neon's Secret UNIverse*, the first book in this brilliant series.